Thomas Roscoe, Silvio Pellico

My Ten Years' Imprisonment

Thomas Roscoe, Silvio Pellico

My Ten Years' Imprisonment

ISBN/EAN: 9783744751254

Printed in Europe, USA, Canada, Australia, Japan

Cover: Foto ©Andreas Hilbeck / pixelio.de

More available books at **www.hansebooks.com**

IMPRISONMENT.

BY

SILVIO PELLICO.

TRANSLATED FROM THE ITALIAN

BY

THOMAS ROSCOE.

NEW YORK:
JOHN B. ALDEN, PUBLISHER.
1889.

INTRODUCTION.

Silvio Pellico was born at Saluzzo, in North Italy, in the year of the fall of the Bastille, 1789. His health as a child was feeble, his temper gentle, and he had the instincts of a poet. Before he was ten years old he had written a tragedy on a theme taken from Macpherson's Ossian. His chief delight as a boy was in acting plays with other children, and he acquired from his father a strong interest in the patriotic movements of the time. He fastened upon French literature during a stay of some years at Lyons with a relation of his mother's. Ugo Foscolo's *Sepolcri* revived his patriotism, and in 1810, at the age of twenty-one, he returned to Italy. He taught French in the Soldiers' Orphans' School at Milan. At Milan he was admitted to the friendship of Vincenzo Monti, a poet then touching his sixtieth year, and of the younger Ugo Foscolo, by whose writings he had been powerfully stirred, and to whom he became closely bound. Silvio Pellico wrote in classical form a tragedy, *Laodicea*, and then, following the national or romantic school, for a famous actress of that time, another tragedy, *Francesca di Rimini*, which was received with great applause.

After the dissolution of the kingdom of Italy, in April 1814, Pellico became tutor to the two children of the Count Porro Lambertenghi, at whose table he met writers of mark, from many countries; Byron (whose *Manfred* he translated), Madame de Stael, Schlegel, Manzoni, and others. In 1819 Silvio Pellico began publishing *Il Conciliatore*, a journal purely literary, that was to look through literature to the life that it expresses, and so help towards the better future of his country. But the merciless excisions of inoffensive passages by the Austrian censorship destroyed the journal in a year.

A secret political association had been formed in Italy of men of all ranks who called themselves the Carbonari (charcoal burners), and who sought the reform of government in Italy. In 1814 they had planned a revolution in Naples, but there was no action until 1820. After successful pressure on the King of the two Sicilies, the forces of the Carbonari under General Pepe entered Naples on the ninth of July, 1820, and King Ferdinand I. swore on the 13th of July to observe the constitution which the Carbonari had proclaimed at Nola and elsewhere during the preceding month. On the twenty-fifth of August, the Austrian government decreed death to every member of a secret society, and *carcere duro e durissimo*, severest pains of imprisonment, to all who had neglected to oppose the progress of Carbonarism. Many seizures were made, and on the 13th of October the gentle editor of the *Conciliatore*, Silvio Pellico, was arrested as a friend of the Carbonari, and taken to the prison of Santa Margherita in Milan.

In the same month of October, the Emperors of Austria and Russia, and the Prince of Prussia met at Troppau to concert measures for crushing the Carbonari.

In January, 1821, they met Ferdinand I. at Laybach and then took arms against Naples. Naples capitulated on the 20th of March, and on the 24th of March, 1821, its Revolutionary council was closed. A decree of April 10th condemned to death all persons who attended meetings of the Carbonari, and the result was a great accession to the strength of this secret society, which spread its branches over Germany and France.

On the 19th of February, 1821, Silvio Pellico was transferred to imprisonment under the leads, on the isle of San Michele, Venice. There he wrote two plays, and some poems. On the 21st of February, 1822, he and his friend Maroncelli were condemned to death; but, their sentence being commuted to twenty years for Maroncelli, and fifteen years for Pellico, of *carcere duro*, they entered their underground prisons at Spielberg on the 10th of April, 1822. The government refused to transmit Pellico's tragedies to his family, lest, though harmless in themselves, the acting of them should bring good-will to a state prisoner. At Spielberg he composed a third tragedy, *Leoniero da Dordona*, though deprived of books, paper, and pens, and preserved it in his memory. In 1825, a rumour of Pellico's death in prison caused great excitement throughout Italy. On the 17th of September, 1830, he was released, by the amnesty of that year, and, avoiding politics thenceforth, devoted himself to religion. The Marchesa Baroli, at Turin, provided for his maintenance, by engaging him as her secretary and librarian. With health made weaker by his sufferings, Silvio Pellico lived on to the age of sixty-five, much honoured by his countrymen. Gioberti dedicated a book to him as "The first of Italian Patriots." He died at Turin on the 1st of February, 1854.

Silvio Pellico's account of his imprisonment, *Le Mie Prigioni*, was first published in Paris in 1833. It has been translated into many languages, and is the work by which he will retain his place in European literature. His other plays, besides the two first named, were *Eufemia di Messina; Iginia di Asti; Leoniero da Dordona*, already named as having been thought out at Spielberg; his *Gismonda; l'Erodiade; Ester d'Engaddi; Corradino;* and a play upon Sir Thomas More. He wrote also poems, *Cantiche*, of which the best are *Eligi e Valfrido* and *Egild;* and, in his last years, a religious manual on the *Duties of Men.*

H. M.

AUTHOR'S PREFACE.

Have I penned these memorials, let me ask myself, from any paltry vanity, or desire to talk about that self? I hope this is not the case, and forasmuch as one may be able to judge in one's own cause, I think I was actuated by better views. These, briefly, were to afford consolation to some unfortunate being, situated like myself, by explaining the evils to which I was exposed, and those sources of relief which I found were accessible, even when labouring under the heaviest misfortune; to bear witness, moreover, that in the midst of my acute and protracted torments, I never found humanity, in the human instruments around me, so hopelessly wicked, so unworthy of consideration, or so barren of noble minds in lowly station, as it is customary to represent it; to engage, if possible, all the generous and good-hearted to love and esteem each other, to become incapable of hating any one; to feel irreconcilable hatred only towards low, base falsehood; cowardice, perfidy, and every kind of moral degradation. It is my object to impress on all that well-known but too often forgotten truth, namely, that both religion and philosophy require calmness of judgment combined with energy of will, and that without such a union, there can be no real justice, no dignity of character, and no sound principles of human action.

MY

TEN YEARS' IMPRISONMENT.

CHAPTER I.

On Friday, the 15th of October, 1820, I was arrested at Milan, and conveyed to the prison of Santa Margherita. The hour was three in the afternoon. I underwent a long examination, which occupied the whole of that and several subsequent days; but of this I shall say nothing. Like some unfortunate lover, harshly dealt with by her he adored, yet resolved to bear it with dignified silence, I leave *la Politica*, such as SHE IS, and proceed to something else.

At nine in the evening of that same unlucky Friday, the actuary consigned me to the jailer, who conducted me to my appointed residence. He there politely requested me to give up my watch, my money, and everything in my pockets, which were to be restored to me in due time; saying which he respectfully bade me good-night.

"Stop, my dear sir," I observed, "I have not yet dined; let me have something to eat."

"Directly; the inn is close by, and you will find the wine good, sir."

"Wine I do not drink."

At this announcement Signor Angiolino gave me a look of unfeigned surprise; he imagined that I was jesting. "Masters of prisons," he rejoined, "who keep shop, have a natural horror of an abstemious captive."

"That may be; I don't drink it."

"I am sorry for you, sir; you will feel solitude twice as heavily."

But perceiving that I was firm, he took his leave; and in half an hour I had something to eat. I took a mouthful, swallowed a glass of water, and found myself alone. My chamber was on the ground floor, and overlooked the court-yard. Dungeons here, dungeons there, to the right, to the left, above, below, and opposite, everywhere met my eye. I leaned against the window, listened to the passing and repassing of the jailers, and the wild song of a number of the unhappy inmates. A century ago, I reflected, and this was a monastery; little then thought the pious, penitent recluses that their cells would now re-echo only to the sounds of blasphemy and licentious song, instead of holy hymn and lamentation from woman's lips; that it would become a dwelling for the wicked of every class—the most part destined to perpetual labour or to the gallows. And in one century to come, what living being will be found in the secells? Oh, mighty Time! unceasing mutability of things! Can he who rightly views your power have reason for regret or despair when Fortune withdraws her smile, when he is made captive, or the scaffold presents itself to his eye? yesterday I thought myself one of the happiest of men; to-day every pleasure, the least flower that strewed my path, has disappeared. Liberty, social converse, the face of my fellow-man, nay, hope itself hath fled. I feel it would be folly to flatter myself; I shall not go hence, except to be thrown into still more horrible receptacles of sorrow; perhaps, bound, into the hands of the executioner. Well, well, the day after my death it will be all one as if I had yielded my spirit in a palace, and been conveyed to the tomb, accompanied with all the pageantry of empty honours.

It was thus, by reflecting on the sweeping speed of time, that I bore up against passing misfortune. Alas, this did not prevent the forms of my father, my mother, two brothers, two sisters, and one other family I had learned to love as if it were my own, from all whom I was, doubtless, for ever cut off, from crossing my mind, and rendering all my philosophical reasoning of no avail. I was unable to resist the thought, and I wept even as a child.

CHAPTER II.

THREE months previous to this time I had gone to Turin, where, after several years of separation, I saw my parents, one of my brothers, and two sisters. We had always been an attached family; no son had ever been more deeply indebted to a father and a mother than I; I remember I was affected at beholding a greater alteration in their looks, the progress of age, than I had expected. I indulged a secret wish to part from them no more, and soothe the pillow of departing age by the grateful cares of a beloved son. How it vexed me, too, I remember, during the few brief days I passed with them, to be compelled by other duties to spend so much of the day from home, and the society of those I had such reason to love and to revere; yes, and I remember now what my mother said one day, with an expression of sorrow, as I went out—"Ah! our Silvio has not come to Turin to see *us!*" The morning of my departure for Milan was a truly painful one. My poor father accompanied me about a mile on my way; and, on leaving me, I more than once turned to look at him, and, weeping, kissed the ring my mother had just given me; nor did I ever before quit my family with a feeling of such painful presentiment. I am not superstitious; but I was astonished at my own weakness, and I more than once exclaimed in a tone of terror, "Good God! whence comes this strange anxiety and alarm?" and, with a sort of inward vision, my mind seemed to behold the approach of some great calamity.

Even yet in prison I retain the impression of that sudden dread and parting anguish, and can recall each word and every look of my distressed parents. The tender reproach of my mother, "Ah! Silvio has not come to Turin to see *us!*" seemed to hang like a weight upon my soul. I regretted a thousand instances in which I might have shown myself more grateful and agreeable to them; I did not even tell them how much I loved; all that I owed to them. I was never to see them more, and yet I turned my eyes with so much like indifference from their dear and venerable features! Why, why was I so chary of giving expression to what I felt (would they could have read it in my looks), to all my gratitude and love? In utter solitude, thoughts like these pierced me to the soul.

I rose, shut the window, and sat some hours, in the idea that it would be in vain to seek repose. At length I threw myself on my pallet, and excessive weariness brought me sleep.

CHAPTER III.

To awake the first night in a prison is a horrible thing. Is it possible, I murmured, trying to collect my thoughts, is it possible I am here? Is not all that passed a dream? Did they really seize me yesterday? Was it I whom they examined from morning till night, who am doomed to the same process day after day, and who wept so bitterly last night when I thought of my dear parents? Slumber, the unbroken silence, and rest had, in restoring my mental powers, added incalculably to the capability of reflecting, and, consequently, of grief. There was nothing to distract my attention; my fancy grew busy with absent forms, and pictured to my eye the pain and terror of my father and mother, and of all dear to me, on first hearing the tidings of my arrest.

At this moment, said I, they are sleeping in peace; or

perhaps, anxiety for me may keep them watching, yet little anticipating the fate to which I am here consigned. Happy for them, were it the will of God, that they should cease to exist ere they hear of this horrible misfortune. Who will give them strength to bear it? Some inward voice seemed to whisper me, He whom the afflicted look up to, love and acknowledge in their hearts; who enabled a mother to follow her son to the mount of Golgotha, and to stand under His cross. He, the friend of the unhappy, the friend of man.

Strange this should be the first time I truly felt the power of religion in my heart: and to filial love did I owe this consolation. Though not ill-disposed, I had hitherto been little impressed with its truth, and had not well adhered to it. All common-place objections I estimated at their just value, yet there were many doubts and sophisms which had shaken my faith. It was long, indeed, since they had ceased to trouble my belief in the existence of the Deity; and persuaded of this, it followed necessarily, as part of His eternal justice, that there must be another life for man who suffers so unjustly here. Hence, I argued, the sovereign reason in man for aspiring to the possession of that second life; and hence, too, a worship founded on the lveo of God, and of his neighbour, and an unceasing impulse to dignify his nature by generous sacrifices. I had already made myself familiar with this doctrine, and I now repeated, "And what else is Christianity but this constant ambition to elevate and dignify our nature?" and I was astonished, when I reflected how pure, how philosophical, and how invulnerable the essence of Christianity manifested itself, that there could come an epoch when philosophy dared to assert, "From this time forth I will stand instead of a religion like this." And in what manner—by inculcating vice? Certainly not. By teaching virtue? Why that will be to teach us to love God and our neighbour; and that is precisely what Christianity has already done, on far higher and purer motives. Yet, notwithstanding such had, for years, been my opinion, I had failed to draw the conclusion, Then be a Christian! No longer let corruption and abuses, the work of man, deter you; no longer make stumbling-blocks of little points of doctrine, since the principal point, made thus irresistibly clear, is to love God and your neighbour.

In prison I finally determined to admit this conclusion, and I admitted it. The fear, indeed, of appearing to others more religious than I had before been, and to yield more to misfortune than to conviction, made me sometimes hesitate; but feeling that I had done no wrong, I felt no debasement, and cared nothing to encounter the possible reproaches I had not deserved, resolving henceforward to declare myself openly a Christian.

CHAPTER IV.

I ADHERED firmly to this resolution as time advanced; but the consideration of it was begun the first night of my captivity. Towards morning the excess of my grief had grown calmer, and I was even astonished at the change. On recalling the idea of my parents and others whom I loved, I ceased to despair of their strength of mind, and the recollection of those virtues which I knew they had long possessed gave me real consolation. Why had I before felt such great dismay on thinking of them, and now so much confidence in their strength of mind? Was this happy change miraculous, or the natural effect of my renewed belief in God? What avails the distinction, while the genuine sublime benefits of religion remain the same.

At midnight two *secondini* (the under jailers are so termed) had paid me a visit, and found me in a very ill mood; in the morning they returned, and were surprised to see me so calm, and even cheerful.

"Last night, sir, you had the face of a basilisk," said Tirola; "now you are quite another thing; I rejoice at it, if, indeed, it be a sign, forgive me the expression, that you are not a scoundrel. Your scoundrels (for I am an old hand at the trade, and my observations are worth something) are always more enraged the second day after their arrest than the first. Do you want some snuff?"

"I do not take it, but will not refuse your offer. If I have not a gorgon-face this morning, it must surely be a proof of my utter insensibility, or easy belief of soon regaining my freedom."

"I should doubt that, even though you were not in durance for state matters. At this time of day they are not so easily got over as you might think; you are not so raw as to imagine such a thing. Pardon me, but you will know more by and by."

"Tell me, how come you to have so pleasant a look, living only, as you do, among the unfortunate?"

"Why, sir, you will attribute it to indifference to others' sufferings; of a truth, I know not how it is; yet, I assure you, it often gives me pain to see the prisoners weep. Truly, I sometimes pretend to be merry to bring a smile upon their faces."

"A thought has just struck me, my friend, which I never had before; it is, that a jailer may be made of very congenial clay."

"Well, the trade has nothing to do with that, sir. Beyond that huge vault you see there, without the court-yard, is another court, and other prisons, all prepared for women. They are, sir, women of a certain class; yet are there some angels among them, as to a good heart. And if you were in my place, sir—"

"I?" and I laughed out heartily.

Tirola was quite disconcerted, and said no more. Perhaps he meant to imply that had I been a *secondino*, it would have been difficult not to become attached to some one or other of these unfortunates.

He now inquired what I wished to take for breakfast, left me, and soon returned with my coffee. I looked hard at him, with a sort of malicious smile, as much as to say, "Would you carry me a bit of a note to an unhappy friend —to my friend Piero?"* He understood it, and answered with another: "No sir; and if you do not take heed how you ask any of my comrades, they will betray you."

Whether or not we understood each other, it is certain I was ten times upon the point of asking him for a sheet of paper, &c.; but there was a something in his eye which seemed to warn me not to confide in any one about me, and still less to others than himself.

CHAPTER V.

HAD Tirola, with his expression of good-nature, possessed a less roguish look, had there been something a little more dignified in his aspect, I should have tried to make him my ambassador; for perhaps a brief communication, if in time, might prevent my friend committing some fatal error, perhaps save him, poor fellow; besides several others, including myself: and too much was already known. Patience! it was fated to be thus.

I was here recalled to be examined anew. The process continued through the day, and was again and again repeated, allowing me only a brief interval during dinner. While this lasted, the time seemed to pass rapidly; the excitement of mind produced by the endless series of questions put to me, and by going over them at dinner and at night, digesting

* Piero Maroncelli da Forli, an excellent poet, and most amiable man, who had also been imprisoned from political motives. The author speaks of him at considerable length, as the companion of his sufferings, in various parts of his work.

all that had been asked and replied to, reflecting on what was likely to come, kept me in a state of incessant activity.

At the end of the first week I had to endure a most vexatious affair. My poor friend Picro, eager as myself to have some communication, sent me a note, not by one of the jailers, but by an unfortunate prisoner who assisted them. He was an old man from sixty to seventy, and condemned to I know not how long a period of captivity. With a pin I had by me I pricked my finger, and scrawled with my blood a few lines in reply, which I committed to the same messenger. He was unluckily suspected, caught with the note upon him, and from the horrible cries that were soon heard, I conjectured that he was severely bastinadoed. At all events I never saw him more.

On my next examination I was greatly irritated to see my note presented to me (luckily containing nothing but a simple salutation), traced in my blood. I was asked how I had contrived to draw the blood; was next deprived of my pin, and a great laugh was raised at the idea and detection of the attempt. Ah, I did not laugh, for the image of the poor old messenger rose before my eyes. I would gladly have undergone any punishment to spare the old man. I could not repress my tears when those piercing cries fell upon my ear. Vainly did I inquire of the jailers respecting his fate. They shook their heads, observing, "He has paid dearly for it, he will never do such like things again; he has a little more rest now." Nor would they speak more fully. Most probably they spoke thus on account of his having died under, or in consequence of, the punishment he had suffered; yet one day I thought I caught a glimpse of him at the further end of the court-yard, carrying a bundle of wood on his shoulders. I felt a beating of the heart as if I had suddenly recognised a brother.

CHAPTER VI.

When I ceased to be persecuted with examinations, and had no longer anything to fill up my time, I felt bitterly the increasing weight of solitude. I had permission to retain a bible, and my Dante; the governor also placed his library at my disposal, consisting of some romances of Scuderi, Piazzi, and worse books still; but my mind was too deeply agitated to apply to any kind of reading whatever. Every day, indeed, I committed a canto of Dante to memory, an exercise so merely mechanical, that I thought more of my own affairs than the lines during their acquisition. The same sort of abstraction attended my perusal of other things, except, occasionally, a few passages of scripture. I had always felt attached to this divine production, even when I had not believed myself one of its avowed followers. I now studied it with far greater respect than before; yet my mind was often almost involuntarily bent upon other matters: and I know not what I read. By degrees I surmounted this difficulty, and was able to reflect upon its great truths with higher relish than I had ever before done. This, in me, did not give rise to the least tendency to moroseness or superstition, nothing being more apt than misdirected devotion to weaken and distort the mind. With the love of God and mankind, it inspired me also with a veneration for justice, and an abhorrence of wickedness, along with a desire of pardoning the wicked. Christianity, instead of militating against anything good, which I had derived from philosophy, strengthened it by the aid of logical deductions, at once more powerful and profound.

Reading one day that it was necessary to pray without ceasing, and that prayer did not consist in many words uttered after the manner of the Pharisees, but in making every word and action accord with the will of God. I determined to commence with earnestness, to pray in the spirit with unceasing effort: in other words, to permit no one thought which should not be inspired by a wish to conform my whole life to the decrees of God.

The forms I adopted were simple and few; not from contempt of them (I think them very salutary, and calculated to excite attention), but from the circumstance of my being unable to go through them at length, without becoming so far abstracted as to make me forget the solemn duty in which I am engaged. This habitual observance of prayer, and the reflection that God is omnipresent as well as omnipotent in His power to save, began ere long to deprive solitude of its horrors, and I often repeated, "Have I not the best society man can have?" and from this period I grew more cheerful, I even sang and whistled in the new joy of my heart. And why lament my captivity? Might not a sudden fever have carried me off? and would my friends then have grieved less over my fate than now? and cannot God sustain them even as He could under a more trying dispensation? And often did I offer up my prayers and fervent hopes that my dear parents might feel, as I myself felt, resigned to my lot; but tears frequently mingled with sweet recollections of home. With all this, my faith in God remained undisturbed, and I was not disappointed.

CHAPTER VII.

To live at liberty is doubtless much better than living in a prison; but, even here, the reflection that God is present with us, that worldly joys are brief and fleeting, and that true happiness is to be sought in the conscience, not in external objects, can give a real zest to life. In less than one month I had made up my mind, I will not say perfectly, but in a tolerable degree, as to the part I should adopt. I saw that, being incapable of the mean action of obtaining impunity by procuring the destruction of others, the only prospect that lay before me was the scaffold, or long protracted captivity. It was necessary that I should prepare myself. I will live, I said to myself, so long as I shall be permitted, and when they take my life, I will do as the unfortunate have done before me ; when arrived at the last moment, I can die. I endeavoured, as much as possible, not to complain, and to obtain every possible enjoyment of mind within my reach. The most customary was that of recalling the many advantages which had thrown a charm round my previous life; the best of fathers, of mothers, excellent brothers and sisters, many friends, a good education, and a taste for letters. Should I now refuse to be grateful to God for all these benefits, because He had pleased to visit me with misfortune? Sometimes, indeed, in recalling past scenes to mind, I was affected even to tears; but I soon recovered my courage and cheerfulness of heart.

At the commencement of my captivity I was fortunate enough to meet with a friend. It was neither the governor, nor any of his under-jailers, nor any of the lords of the process-chamber. Who then?—a poor deaf and dumb boy, five or six years old, the offspring of thieves, who had paid the penalty of the law. This wretched little orphan was supported by the police, with several other boys in the same condition of life. They all dwelt in a room opposite my own, and were only permitted to go out at certain hours to breathe a little air in the yard. Little deaf and dumb used to come under my window, smiled, and made his obeisance to me. I threw him a piece of bread; he took it, and gave a leap of joy, then ran to his companions, divided it, and returned to eat his own share under the window. The others gave me a wistful look from a distance, but ventured no nearer, while the deaf and dumb boy expressed a sympathy for me; not, I found, affected, out of mere selfishness. Sometimes he was at a loss what to do with the bread I gave him, and made signs that he had eaten enough, as also his companions. When he saw one of the under-jailers going into my room, he would give him what he had got from me, in order to restore it to me. Yet he continued to haunt my window, and seemed rejoiced whenever I deigned to notice him. One day the jailer permitted him to enter my prison, when he instantly ran to embrace my knees, actually uttering a cry of joy. I took him up in my arms, and he threw his little hands about my neck, and lavished on me the tenderest caresses. How much affection in his smile and manner! how eagerly I longed to have him to educate, raise him from his abject condition, and snatch him, perhaps, from utter ruin. I never even learnt his name; he did not himself know that he had one. He seemed always happy, and I never saw him weep except once, and that was on being beaten, I know not why, by the jailer. Strange that he should be thus happy in a receptacle of so much pain and sorrow; yet he was light-hearted as the son of a grandee. From him I learnt, at least, that the mind need not depend on situation, but may be rendered independent of external things. Govern the imagination, and we shall be well, wheresoever we happen to be placed. A day is soon over, and if at night we can retire to rest without actual pain and hunger, it little matters whether it be within the walls of a prison, or of a kind of building which they call a palace. Good reasoning this; but how are we to contrive so to govern the imagination? I began to try, and sometimes I thought I had succeeded to a miracle; but at others the enchantress triumphed, and I was unexpectedly astonished to find tears starting into my eyes.

CHAPTER VIII.

I AM so far fortunate, I often said, that they have given me a dungeon on the ground floor, near the court, where that dear boy comes within a few steps of me, to converse in our own mute language. We made immense progress in it; we expressed a thousand various feelings I had no idea we could do, by the natural expressions of the eye, the gesture, and the whole countenance. Wonderful human intelligence! How graceful were his motions! how beautiful his smile! how quickly he corrected whatever expression I saw of his that seemed to displease me! How well he understands I love him, when he plays with any of his companions! Standing only at my window to observe him, it seemed as if I possessed a kind of influence over his mind, favourable to his education. By dint of repeating the mutual exercise of signs, we should be enabled to perfect the communication of our ideas. The more instruction he gets, the more gentle and kind he becomes, the more he will be attached to me. To him I shall be the genius of reason and of good; he will learn to confide his sorrows to me, his pleasures, all he feels and wishes; I will console, elevate, and direct him in his whole conduct. It may be that this my lot may be protracted from month to month, even till I grow grey in my captivity. Perhaps this little child may continue to grow under my eye, and become one in the service of this large family of pain, and grief, and calamity. With such a disposition as he has already shown, what would become of him? Alas; he would at most be made only a good under-keeper, or fill some similar place. Yet I shall surely have conferred on him some benefit if I can succeed in giving him a desire to do kind offices to the good and to himself, and to nourish sentiments of habitual benevolence. This soliloquy was very natural in my situation; I was always fond of children, and the office of an instructor appeared to me a sublime duty. For a few years I had acted in that capacity with Giacomo and Giulio Porro, two young men of noble promise, whom I loved, and shall continue to love as if they were my own sons. Often while in prison were my thoughts busied with them; and how it grieved me not to be enabled to complete their education. I sincerely prayed that they might meet with a new master, who would be as much attached to them as I had been.

At times I could not help exclaiming to myself, What a strange burlesque is all this! instead of two noble youths, rich in all that nature and fortune can endow them with, here I have a pupil, poor little fellow! deaf, dumb, a castaway; the son of a robber, who at most can aspire only to the rank of an under-jailer, and which, in a little less softened phraseology, would mean to say a *sbirro.** This reflection confused and disquieted me; yet hardly did I hear the *strillo* † of my little dummy than I felt my heart grow warm again, just as a father when he hears the voice of a son. I lost all anxiety about his mean estate. It is no fault of his if he be lopped of Nature's fairest proportions. and was born the son of a robber. A humane, generous heart, in an age of innocence, is always respectable. I looked on him, therefore, from day to day with increased affection, and was more than ever desirous of cultivating his good qualities, and his growing intelligence. Nay, perhaps we might both live to get out of prison, when I would establish him in the college for the deaf and dumb, and thus open for him a path more fortunate and pleasing than to play the part of a *sbirro.* Whilst thus pleasingly engaged in meditating his future welfare, two of the under-jailers one day walked into my cell.

"You must change your quarters, sir!"

"What mean you by that?"

"We have orders to remove you into another chamber."

"Why so?"

"Some other great bird has been caged, and this being the better apartment—you understand."

"Oh, yes! it is the first resting-place for the newly arrived."

* A bailiff. † A sort of scream peculiar to dumb children.

They conveyed me to the opposite side of the court, where I could no longer converse with my little deaf and dumb friend, and was far removed from the ground floor. In walking across, I beheld the poor boy sitting on the ground, overcome with grief and astonishment, for he knew he had lost me. Ere I quite disappeared, he ran towards me; my conductors tried to drive him away, but he reached me, and I caught him in my arms, and returned his caresses with expressions of tenderness I sought not to conceal. I tore myself from him, and entered my new abode.

CHAPTER IX.

It was a dark and gloomy place; instead of glass it had pasteboard for the windows; the walls were rendered more repulsive by being hung with some wretched attempts at painting, and when free from this lugubrious colour, were covered with inscriptions. These last gave the name and country of many an unhappy inmate, with the date of the fatal day of their captivity. Some consisted of lamentations on the perfidy of false friends, denouncing their own folly, or women, or the judge who condemned them. Among a few were brief sketches of the victims' lives; still fewer embraced moral maxims. I found the following words of Pascal: "Let those who attack religion learn first what religion is. Could it boast of commanding a direct view of the Deity, without veil or mystery, it would be to attack that religion to say, 'that there is nothing seen in the world which displays Him with such clear evidence.' But since it rather asserts that man is involved in darkness, far from God, who is hidden from human knowledge, insomuch as to give Himself the name in scripture of '*Deus absconditus*,' what advantage can the enemies of religion derive when, neglecting, as they profess to do, the science of truth, they complain that the truth is not made apparent to them?"

Lower down was written (the words of the same author), "It is not here a question of some trivial interest relating to a stranger; it applies to ourselves, and to all we possess. The immortality of the soul is a question of that deep and momentous importance to all, as to imply an utter loss of reason to rest totally indifferent as to the truth or the fallacy of the proposition." Another inscription was to this effect: "I bless the hour of my imprisonment; it has taught me to know the ingratitude of man, my own frailty, and the goodness of God." Close to these words again appeared the proud and desperate imprecations of one who signed himself an Atheist, and who launched his impieties against the Deity, as if he had forgotten that he had just before said there was no God. Then followed another column, reviling the cowardly fools, as they were termed, whom captivity had converted into fanatics. I one day pointed out these strange impieties to one of the jailers, and inquired who had written them? "I am glad I have found this," was the reply, "there are so many of them, and I have so little time to look for them;" and he took his knife, and began to erase it as fast as he could.

"Why do you do that?" I inquired of him.

"Because the poor devil who wrote it was condemned to death for a cold-blooded murder; he repented, and made us promise to do him this kindness."

"Heaven pardon him!" I exclaimed; "what was it he did?"

"Why, as he found he could not kill his enemy, he revenged himself by slaying the man's son, one of the finest boys you ever saw."

I was horror-struck. Could ferocity of disposition proceed to such lengths? and could a monster, capable of such a deed, hold the insulting language of a man superior to all human weaknesses? to murder the innocent, and a child!

CHAPTER X.

In my new prison, black and filthy to an extreme, I sadly missed the society of my little dumb friend. I stood for hours in anxious, weary mood, at the window which looked over a gallery, on the other side of which could be seen the extremity of the court-yard, and the window of my former cell. Who had succeeded me there? I could discern his figure, as he paced quickly to and fro, apparently in violent agitation. Two or three days subsequently, I perceived that he had got writing materials, and remained busied at his little table the whole of the day. At length I recognised him. He came forth accompanied by his jailer; he was going to be examined, when I saw he was no other than Melchiorre Gioja.* It went to my heart:—"You, too, noble, excellent man, have not escaped!" Yet he was more fortunate than I. After a few months' captivity, he regained his liberty. To behold any really estimable being always does me good; it affords me pleasant matter for reflection, and for esteem—both of great advantage. I could have laid down my life to save such a man from captivity; yet merely to see him was some consolation to me. After regarding him intently, some time, to ascertain if he were tranquil or agitated, I offered up a heart-felt prayer for his deliverance; I felt my spirits revived, a greater flow of ideas, and greater satisfaction with myself.

* Melchiorre Gioja, a native of Piacenza, was one of the most profound writers of our times, principally upon subjects of public economy. Being suspected of carrying on a secret correspondence, he was arrested in 1820, and imprisoned for a space of nine months. Among the more celebrated of his works are those entitled, *Nuovo prospetto delle Scienze Economiche, Trattato del Merito e delle Ricompense, Dell' Ingiuria e dei Danni, Filosofia della Statistica, Ideologia e Esercizo Logico, Delle Manifatture, Del Divorzio, Elementi di Filosofia, Nuovo Galateo, Qual Governo convenga all' Italia.* This able writer died in the month of January, 1829.

Such an incident as this has a charm for utter solitude, of which you can form no idea without experiencing it. A poor dumb boy had before supplied me with this real enjoyment, and I now derived it from a distant view of a man of distinguished merit.

Perhaps some one of the jailers had informed, him where I was. One morning, on opening his window, he waved his handkerchief in token of salutation, and I replied in the same manner. I need not describe the pleasure I felt; it appeared as if we were no longer separated; and we discoursed in the silent intercourse of the spirit, which, when every other medium is cut off, in the least look, gesture, or signal of any kind, can make itself comprehended and felt.

It was with no small pleasure I anticipated a continuation of this friendly communication. Day after day, however, went on, and I was never more gratified by the appearance of the same favourite signals. Yet I frequently saw my friend at his window; I waved my handkerchief, but in vain; he answered it no more. I was now informed by our jailers, that Gioja had been strictly prohibited from exciting my notice, or replying to it in any manner. Notwithstanding, he still continued to look at me, and I at him, and in this way, we conversed upon a great variety of subjects, which helped to keep us alive.

CHAPTER XI.

Along the same gallery, upon a level with my prison, I saw other prisoners passing and repassing the whole day to the place of examination. They were, for the chief part, of lowly condition, but occasionally one or two of better rank. All, however, attracted my attention, brief as was the sight of them, and I truly compassionated them. So sorrowful a spectacle for some time filled me with grief, but by degrees I became habituated to it, and at last it rather relieved than added to the horror of my solitude. A number of women, also, who had been arrested, passed by. There was a way from the gallery, through a large vault, leading to another court, and in that part were placed the female prisoners, and others labouring under disease. A single wall, and very slight, separated my dwelling from that of some of the women. Sometimes I was almost deafened with their songs, at others with their bursts of maddened mirth. Late at evening, when the din of day had ceased, I could hear them conversing, and, had I wished, I could easily have joined with them. Was it timidity, pride, or prudence which restrained me from all communication with the unfortunate and degraded of their sex? Perhaps it partook of all, Woman, when she is what she ought to be, is for me a creature so admirable, so sublime, the mere seeing, hearing, and speaking to her, enriches my mind with such noble fantasies; but rendered vile and despicable, she disturbs, she afflicts, she deprives my heart, as it were, of all its poetry and its love. Spite of this, there were among those feminine voices, some so very sweet that, there is no use in denying it, they were dear to me. One in particular surpassed the rest; I heard it more seldom, and it uttered nothing unworthy of its fascinating tone. She sung little. and mostly kept repeating these two pathetic lines :—

Chi rende alla meschina
La sua felicità?

Ah, who will give the lost one
Her vanished dream of bliss?

At other times, she would sing from the litany. Her companions joined with her; but still I could discern the voice of Maddalene from all others, which seemed only to unite for the purpose of robbing me of it. Sometimes, too, when her companions were recounting to her their various misfortunes, I could hear her pitying them; could catch even her very sighs, while she invariably strove to console them: "Courage, courage, my poor dear," she one day said, "God is very good, and He will not abandon us."

How could I do otherwise than imagine she was beautiful, more unfortunate than guilty, naturally virtuous, and capable of reformation? Who would blame me because I was affected with what she said, listened to her with respect, and offered up my prayers for her with more than usual earnestness of heart. Innocence is sacred, and repentance ought to be equally respected. Did the most perfect of men, the Divinity on earth, refuse to cast a pitying eye on weak, sinful women; to respect their fear and confusion, and rank them among the minds he delighted to consort with and to honour? By what law, then, do we act, when we treat with so much contempt women fallen into ignominy?

While thus reasoning, I was frequently tempted to raise my voice and speak, as a brother in misfortune, to poor Maddalene. I had often even got out the first syllable; and how strange! I felt my heart beat like an enamoured youth of fifteen; I who had reached thirty-one; and it seemed as if I should never be able to pronounce the name, till I cried out almost in a rage, "Mad! Mad!" yes, mad enough, thought I.

CHAPTER XII.

THUS ended my romance with that poor unhappy one; yet it did not fail to produce me many sweet sensations during several weeks. Often, when steeped in melancholy, would her sweet calm voice breathe consolation to my spirit; when, dwelling on the meanness and ingratitude of mankind, I became irritated, and hated the world, the voice of Maddalene gently led me back to feelings of compassion and indulgence.

How I wish, poor, unknown, kind-hearted repentant one,

that no heavy punishment may befall thee. And whatever thou shalt suffer, may it well avail thee, re-dignify thy nature, and teach thee to live and die to thy Saviour and thy Lord. Mayest thou meet compassion and respect from all around thee, as thou didst from me a stranger to thee. Mayest thou teach all who see thee thy gentle lesson of patience, sweetness, the love of virtue, and faith in God, with which thou didst inspire him who loved without having beheld thee. Perhaps I erred in thinking thee beautiful, but, sure I am, thou didst wear the beauty of the soul. Thy conversation, though spoken amidst grossness and corruption of every kind, was ever chaste and graceful; whilst others imprecated, thou didst bless; when eager in contention, thy sweet voice still pacified, like oil upon the troubled waters. If any noble mind hath read thy worth, and snatched thee from an evil career; hath assisted thee with delicacy, and wiped the tears from thy eyes, may every reward heaven can give be his portion, that of his children, and of his children's children!

Next to mine was another prison occupied by several men. I also heard *their* conversation. One seemed of superior authority, not so much probably from any difference of rank, as owing to greater eloquence and boldness. He played, what may musically be termed, the first fiddle. He stormed himself, yet put to silence those who presumed to quarrel by his imperious voice. He dictated the tone of the society, and after some feeble efforts to throw off his authority they submitted, and gave the reins into his hands.

There was not a single one of those unhappy men who had a touch of that in him to soften the harshness of prison hours, to express one kindly sentiment, one emanation of religion, or of love. The chief of these neighbours of mine saluted me, and I replied. He asked me how I contrived to pass *such a cursed dull life?* I answered, that it was melancholy, to be sure; but no life was a cursed one to me, and that to our last hour, it was best to do all to procure oneself the pleasure of thinking and of loving.

"Explain, sir, explain what you mean!"

I explained, but was not understood. After many ingenious attempts, I determined to clear it up in the form of example, and had the courage to bring forward the extremely singular and moving effect produced upon me by the voice of Maddalene; when the magisterial head of the prison burst into a violent fit of laughter. "What is all that, what is that?" cried his companions. He then repeated my words with an air of burlesque; peals of laughter followed, and I there stood, in their eyes, the picture of a convicted blockhead.

As it is in prison, so it is in the world. Those who make it their wisdom to go into passions, to complain, to defy, to abuse, think that to pity, to love, to console yourself with gentle and beautiful thoughts and images, in accord with humanity and its great Author, is all mere folly.

CHAPTER XIII.

I LET them laugh and said not a word; they hit at me again two or three times, but I was mute. "He will come no more near the window," said one, "he will hear nothing but the sighs of Maddalene; we have offended him with laughing." At length, the chief imposed silence upon the whole party, all amusing themselves at my expense. "Silence, beasts as you are; devil a bit you know what you are talking about. Our neighbour is none so long eared an animal as you imagine. You do not possess the power of reflection, no not you. I grin and joke; but afterwards I reflect. Every low-born clown can stamp and roar, as we do here. Grant a little more real cheerfulness, a spark more of charity, a bit more faith in the blessing of heaven;—what do you imagine that all this would be a sign of?" "Now, that I also reflect," replied one, "I fancy it would be a sign of being a little less of a brute."

"Bravo!" cried his leader, in a most stentorian howl! "now I begin to have some hope of you."

I was not overproud at being thus rated *a little less of a brute* than the rest; yet I felt a sort of pleasure that these wretched men had come to some agreement as to the importance of cultivating, in some degree, more benevolent sentiments,

I again approached the window, the chief called me, and I answered, hoping that I might now moralise with him in my own way. I was deceived; vulgar minds dislike serious reasoning; if some noble truth start up, they applaud for a moment, but the next withdraw their notice, or scruple not to attempt to shine by questioning, or aiming to place it in some ludicrous point of view.

I was next asked if I were imprisoned for debt?

"No."

"Perhaps you are paying the penalty of a false oath, then?"

"No, it is quite a different thing."

"An affair of love, most likely, I guess?"

"No."

"You have killed a man, mayhap?"

"No."

"It's for carbonarism, then?"

"Exactly so."

"And who are these carbonari?"

"I know so little of them, I cannot tell you."

Here a jailer interrupted us in great anger; and after commenting on the gross improprieties committed by my neighbours, he turned towards me, not with the gravity of a *sbirro*, but the air of a master: "For shame, sir, for shame! to think of talking to men of this stamp! do you know, sir, that they are all robbers?"

I reddened up, and then more deeply for having shown I blushed. and methought that to deign to converse with the unhappy of however lowly rank, was rather a mark of goodness than a fault.

CHAPTER XIV.

NEXT morning I went to my window to look for Melchiorre Gioja; but conversed no more with the robbers. I replied to their salutation, and added, that I had been forbidden to hold conversation. The secretary who had presided at my examinations, told me with an air of mystery, I was about to receive a visit. After a little further preparation, he acquainted me that it was my father; and so saying, bade me follow him. I did so, in a state of great agitation, assuming at the same time an appearance of perfect calmness in order not to distress my unhappy parent. Upon first hearing of my arrest, he had been led to suppose it was for some trifling affair, and that I should soon be set at liberty. Finding his mistake, however, he had now come to solicit the Austrian government on my account. Here, too, he deluded himself, for he never imagined I could have been rash enough to expose myself to the penalty of the laws, and the cheerful tone in which I now spoke persuaded him that there was nothing very serious in the business.

The few words that were permitted to pass between us, gave me indescribable pain; the more so from the restraint I had placed upon my feelings. It was yet more difficult at the moment of parting. In the existing state of things, as regarded Italy, I felt convinced that Austria would make some fearful examples, and that I should be condemned either to death or long protracted imprisonment. It was my object to conceal this from my father and to flatter his hopes at a moment when I was inquiring for a mother, brother, and sisters, whom I never expected to behold more. Though I knew it to be impossible, I even calmly requested of him that he would come and see me again, while my heart was wrung with the bitter conflict of my feelings. He took his leave, filled with the same agreeable delusion, and I painfully retraced my steps back into my dungeon. I thought that solitude would now be a relief to me; that to weep would somewhat ease my burdened heart? yet, strange to say, I could not shed a tear. The extreme wretchedness of feeling this inability even to shed tears excites, under some of the heaviest calamities, is the severest trial of all, and I have often experienced it.

An acute fever, attended by severe pains in my head, followed this interview. I could not take any nourishment; and I often said, how happy it would be for me, were it indeed to prove mortal. Foolish and cowardly wish! heaven refused to hear my prayer, and I now feel grateful that it did. Though a stern teacher, adversity fortifies the mind, and renders man what he seems to have been intended for; at least, a good man, a being capable of struggling with difficulty and danger; presenting an object not unworthy, even in the eyes of the old Romans, of the approbation of the gods.

CHAPTER XV.

Two days afterwards I again saw my father. I had rested well the previous night, and was free from fever; before him I preserved the same calm and even cheerful deportment, so that no one could have suspected I had recently suffered, and still continued to suffer so much. "I am in hopes," observed my father, "that within a very few days we shall see you at Turin. Your mother has got your old room in readiness, and we are all expecting you to come. Pressing affairs now call me away, but lose no time, I entreat you, in preparing to rejoin us once more." His kind and affecting expressions added to my grief. Compassion and filial piety, not unmingled with a species of remorse, induced me to feign assent; yet afterwards I reflected how much more worthy it had been, both of my father and myself, to have frankly told him that most probably, we should never see each other again, at least in this world. Let us take farewell like men, without a murmur and without a tear, and let me receive the benediction of a father before I die. As regarded myself, I should wish to have adopted language like that; but when I gazed on his aged and venerable features, and his grey hairs, something seemed to whisper me, that it would be too much for the affectionate old man to bear; and the words died in my heart. Good God! I thought, should he know the extent of the *evil*, he might, perhaps, run distracted, such is his extreme attachment to me: he might fall at my feet, or even expire before my eyes. No! I could not tell him the truth, nor so much as prepare him for it; we shed not a tear, and he took his departure in the same pleasing delusion as before. On returning into my dungeon I was seized in the same manner, and with still more aggravated suffering, as I had been after the last interview; and, as then, my anguish found no relief from tears.

I had nothing now to do but resign myself to all the horrors of long captivity, and to the sentence of death. But to prepare myself to bear the idea of the immense load of grief that must fall on every dear member of my family, on learning my lot, was beyond my power. It haunted me like a spirit, and to fly from it I threw myself on my knees, and in a passion of devotion uttered aloud the following prayer:—"My God! from thy hand I will accept all—for me all: but deign most wonderfully to strengthen the hearts of those to whom I was so very dear! Grant thou that I may cease to be such to them now: and that not the life of the least of them may be shortened by their care for me, even by a single day!"

Strange! wonderful power of prayer! for several hours my mind was raised to a contemplation of the Deity, and my confidence in His goodness proportionately increased; I meditated also on the dignity of the human mind when, freed from selfishness, it exerts itself to will only that which is the will of eternal wisdom. This *can* be done, and it is man's duty to do it. Reason, which is the voice of the Deity, teaches us that it is right to submit to every sacrifice for the sake of virtue. And how could the sacrifice which we owe to virtue be completed, if in the most trying afflictions we struggle against the will of Him who is the source of all virtue? When death on the scaffold, or any other species of martyrdom becomes inevitable, it is a proof of wretched degradation, or ignorance, not to be able to approach it with blessing upon our lips. Nor is it only necessary we should submit to death, but to the affliction which we know those most dear to us must suffer on our account. All it is lawful for us to ask is, that God will temper such affliction, and that he will direct us all, for such a prayer is always sure to be accepted.

CHAPTER XVI.

For a period of some days I continued in the same state of mind; a sort of calm sorrow, full of peace, affection, and religious thoughts. I seemed to have overcome every weakness, and as if I were no longer capable of suffering new anxiety. Fond delusion! it is man's duty to aim at reaching as near to perfection as possible, though he can never attain it here. What now disturbed me was the sight of an unhappy friend, my good Piero, who passed along the gallery within a few yards of me, while I stood at my window. They were removing him from his cell into the prison destined for criminals. He was hurried by so swiftly that I had barely time to recognise him, and to receive and return his salutation.

Poor young man! in the flower of his age, with a genius

of high promise, of frank, upright, and most affectionate disposition, born with a keen zest of the pleasures of existence, to be at once precipitated into a dungeon, without the remotest hope of escaping the severest penalty of the laws. So great was my compassion for him, and my regret at being unable to afford him the slightest consolation, that it was long before I could recover my composure of mind. I knew how tenderly he was attached to every member of his numerous family, how deeply interested in promoting their happiness, and how devotedly his affection was returned. I was sensible what must be the affliction of each and all under so heavy a calamity. Strange, that though I had just reconciled myself to the idea in my own case, a sort of phrensy seized my mind when I depicted the scene; and it continued so long that I began to despair of mastering it.

Dreadful as this was, it was still but an illusion. Ye afflicted ones, who believe yourselves victims of some irresistible, heart-rending, and increasing grief, suffer a little while with patience, and you will be undeceived. Neither perfect peace, nor utter wretchedness can be of long continuance here below. Recollect this truth, that you may not become unduly elevated in prosperity, and despicable under the trials which assuredly await you. A sense of weariness and apathy succeeded the terrible excitement I had undergone. But indifference itself is transitory, and I had some fear lest I should continue to suffer without relief under these wretched extremes of feeling. Terrified at the prospect of such a future, I had recourse once more to the only Being from whom I could hope to receive strength to bear it, and devoutly bent down in prayer. I beseeched the Father of mercies to befriend my poor deserted Piero, even as myself, and to support his family no less than my own. By constant repetition of prayers like these, I became perfectly calm and resigned.

CHAPTER XVII.

It was then I reflected upon my previous violence; I was angry at my own weakness and folly, and sought means of remedying them. I had recourse to the following expedient. Every morning, after I had finished my devotions, I set myself diligently to work to recall to mind every possible occurrence of a trying and painful kind, such as a final parting from my dearest friends and the approach of the executioner. I did this not only in order to inure my nerves to bear sudden or dreadful incidents, too surely my future portion, but that I might not again be taken unawares. At first this melancholy task was insupportable, but I persevered; and in a short time became reconciled to it.

In the spring of 1821 Count Luigi Porro * obtained permission to see me. Our warm friendship, the eagerness to communicate our mutual feelings, and the restraint imposed by the presence of an imperial secretary, with the brief time allowed us, the presentiments I indulged, and our efforts to appear calm, all led me to expect that I should be thrown into a state of fearful excitement, worse than I had yet suffered. It was not so; after taking his leave I remained calm; such to me proved the signal efficacy of

* The Count Luigi Porro was one of the most distinguished men of Milan, and remarkable for the zeal and liberality with which he promoted the cultivation of literature and the arts. Having early remarked the excellent disposition of the youthful Pellico, the Count invited him to reside in his mansion, and take upon himself the education of his sons, uniformly considering him, at the same time, more in the light of a friend than of a dependent. Count Porro himself subsequently fell under the suspicions of the Austrian Government, and having betaken himself to flight, was twice condemned to death (as contumacious), the first time under the charge of *Carbonarism*, and the second time for a pretended conspiracy. The sons of Count Porro are more than once alluded to by their friend and tutor, as the author designates himself.

guarding against the assault of sudden and violent emotions. The task I set myself to acquire, constant calmness of mind, arose less from a desire to relieve my unhappiness than from a persuasion how undignified, unworthy, and injurious, was a temper opposite to this, I mean a continued state of excitement and anxiety. An excited mind ceases to reason; carried away by a resistless torrent of wild ideas, it forms for itself a sort of mad logic, full of anger and malignity; it is in a state at once as absolutely unphilosophical as it is unchristian.

If I were a divine I should often insist upon the necessity of correcting irritability and inquietude of character; none can be truly good without that be effected. How nobly pacific, both with regard to himself and others, was He whom we are all bound to imitate. There is no elevation of mind, no justice without moderation in principles and ideas, without a pervading spirit which inclines us rather to smile at, than fall into a passion with, the events of this little life. Anger is never productive of any good, except in the extremely rare case of being employed to humble the wicked, and to terrify them from pursuing the path of crime, even as the usurers were driven by an angry Saviour, from polluting his holy Temple. Violence and excitement, perhaps, differing altogether from what I felt, are no less blamable. Mine was the mania of despair and affliction: I felt a disposition, while suffering under its horrors, to hate and to curse mankind. Several individuals, in particular, appeared to my imagination depicted in the most revolting colours. It is a sort of moral epidemic, I believe, springing from vanity and selfishness; for when a man despises and detests his fellow-creatures, he necessarily assumes that he is much better than the rest of the world. The doctrine of such men amounts to this:—"Let us admire only one another, if we turn the rest of mankind into a mere mob, we shall appear like demi-gods on earth." It is a curious fact that living in a state of hostility and rage actually affords pleasure; it seems as if people thought there was a species of heroism in it. If, unfortunately, the object of our wrath happens to die, we lose no time in finding some one to fill the vacant place. Whom shall I attack next, whom shall I hate? Ah! is that the villain I was looking out for? What a prize! Now my friends, at him, give him no quarter. Such is the world, and, without uttering a libel, I may add that it is not what it ought to be.

CHAPTER XVIII.

It showed no great malignity, however, to complain of the horrible place in which they had incarcerated me, but fortunately another room became vacant, and I was agreeably surprised on being informed that I was to have it. Yet strangely enough, I reflected with regret that I was about to leave the vicinity of Maddalene. Instead of feeling rejoiced, I mourned over it with almost childish feeling. I had always attached myself to some object, even from motives comparatively slight. On leaving my horrible abode, I cast back a glance at the heavy wall against which I had so often supported myself, while listening as closely as possible to the gentle voice of the repentant girl. I felt a desire to hear, if only for the last time, those two pathetic lines,—

> Chi rende alla meschina
> La sua felicità?

Vain hope! here was another separation in the short period of my unfortunate life. But I will not go into any further details, lest the world should laugh at me, though it would be hypocrisy in me to affect to conceal that, for several days after, I felt melancholy at this imaginary parting.

While going out of my dungeon I also made a farewell signal to two of the robbers, who had been my neighbours, and who were then standing at their window. Their chief also got notice of my departure, ran to the window, and repeatedly saluted me. He began likewise to sing the little air, *Chi rende alla meschina;* and was this, thought I, merely to ridicule me? No doubt that forty out of fifty would say decidedly, "It was!" In spite, however, of being outvoted, I incline to the opinion that the *good robber* meant it kindly; and, as such I received it, and gave him a look of thanks. He saw it, and thrust his arm through the bars, and waved his cap, nodding kindly to me as I turned to go down the stairs.

Upon reaching the yard below, I was further consoled by a sight of the little deaf and dumb boy. He saw me, and instantly ran towards me with a look of unfeigned delight. The wife of the jailer, however, Heaven knows why, caught hold of the little fellow, and rudely thrusting him back, drove him into the house. I was really vexed; and yet the resolute little efforts he made even then to reach me, gave me indescribable pleasure at the moment, so pleasing it is to find that one is really loved. This was a day full of great adventures for *me;* a few steps further I passed the window of my old prison, now the abode of Gioja: "How are you, Melchiorre?" I exclaimed as I went by. He raised his head, and getting as near me as it was *possible*, cried out, "How do you do, Silvio?" They would not let me stop a single moment; I passed through the great gate, ascended a flight of stairs, which brought us to a large, well-swept room, exactly over that occupied by Gioja. My bed was brought after me, and I was then left to myself by my conductors. My first object was to examine the walls; I met with several inscriptions, some written with charcoal, others in pencil, and a few incised with some sharp point. I remember there were some very pleasing verses in French, and I am sorry I forgot to commit them to mind. They were signed "The duke of Normandy." I tried to sing them, adapting to them, as well as I could, the favourite air of my poor Maddalene. What was my surprise to hear a voice, close to me, reply in the same words, sung to another air. When he had finished, I cried out, "Bravo!" and he saluted me with great respect, inquiring if I were a Frenchman.

"No; an Italian, and my name is Silvio Pellico."

"The author of *Francesca da Rimini?*" *

"The same."

Here he made me a fine compliment, following it with the condolences usual on such occasions, upon hearing I had been committed to prison. He then inquired of what part of Italy I was a native. "Piedmont," was the reply; "I am from Saluzzo." Here I was treated to another compliment, on the character and genius of the Piedmontese, in particular, the celebrated men of Saluzzo, at the head of whom he ranked Bodoni.* All this was said in an easy refined tone, which showed the man of the world, and one who had received a good education.

"Now, may I be permitted," said I, "to inquire who *you* are, sir?"

* This excellent tragedy, suggested by the celebrated episode in the fifth canto of Dante's *Inferno*, was received by the whole of Italy with the most marked applause. Such a production at once raised the young author to a high station in the list of Italy's living poets.

† The Cavalier Giovanni Bodoni was one of the most distinguished among modern printers. Becoming admirably skilled in his art, and in the oriental languages, acquired in the college of the Propaganda at Rome, he went to the Royal Printing Establishment at Parma, of which he took the direction in 1813, and in which he continued till the period of his death. In the list of the numerous works which he thence gave to the world may be mentioned the *Pater Noster Poliglotto*, the *Iliad* in Greek, the *Epithalamia Exoticis*, and the *Manuale Tipografico*, works which will maintain their reputation to far distant times

"I heard you singing one of my little songs," was the reply.

"What! the two beautiful stanzas upon the wall are yours!"

"They are, sir."

"You are, therefore, ——"

"The unfortunate duke of Normandy."

CHAPTER XIX.

The jailer at that moment passed under our windows, and ordered us to be silent.

What can he mean by the unfortunate duke of Normandy? thought I, musing to myself. Ah! is not that the title said to be assumed by the son of Louis XVI.? but that unhappy child is indisputably no more. Then my neighbour must be one of those unlucky adventurers who have undertaken to bring him to life again. Not a few had already taken upon themselves to personate this Louis XVII., and were proved to be impostors; how is my new acquaintance entitled to greater credit for his pains?

Although I tried to give him the advantage of a doubt, I felt an insurmountable incredulity upon the subject, which was not subsequently removed. At the same time, I determined not to mortify the unhappy man, whatever sort of absurdity he might please to hazard before my face.

A few minutes afterwards he began again to sing, and we soon renewed our conversation. In answer to my inquiry, "What is your real name?" he replied, "I am no other than Louis XVII." And he then launched into very severe invectives against his uncle, Louis XVIII., the usurper of his just and natural rights.

"But why," said I, "did you not prefer your claims at the period of the restoration?"

"I was unable, from extreme illness, to quit the city of Bologna. The moment I was better I hastened to Paris; I presented myself to the allied monarchs, but the work was done. The good Prince of Condé knew, and received me with open arms, but his friendship availed me not. One evening, passing through a lonely street, I was suddenly attacked by assassins, and escaped with difficulty. After wandering through Normandy, I returned into Italy, and stopped some time at Modena. Thence I wrote to the allied powers, in particular to the Emperor Alexander, who replied to my letter with expressions of the greatest kindness. I did not then despair of obtaining justice, or, at all events, if my rights were to be sacrificed, of being allowed a decent provision, becoming a prince. But I was arrested, and handed over to the Austrian government. During eight months I have been here buried alive, and God knows when I shall regain my freedom."

I begged him to give me a brief sketch of his life. He told me very minutely what I already knew relating to Louis XVII. and the cruel Simon, and of the infamous calumnies that wretch was induced to utter respecting the unfortunate queen, &c. Finally he said, that while in prison, some persons came with an idiot boy of the name of Mathurin, who was substituted for him, while he himself was carried off. A coach and four was in readiness; one of the horses was merely a wooden-machine, in the interior of which he was concealed. Fortunately, they reached the confines, and the General (he gave me the name, which has escaped me) who effected his release, educated him for some time with the attention of a father, and subsequently sent, or accompanied him, to America. There the young king, without a sceptre, had room to indulge his wandering disposition; he was half famished in the forests; became at length a soldier, and resided some time, in good credit, at the court of the Brazils. There, too, he was pursued and persecuted, till compelled to make his escape. He returned to Europe towards the close of Napoleon's career, was kept a close prisoner at Naples by Murat; and, at last, when he was liberated, and in full preparation to reclaim the throne of France, he was seized with that unlucky illness at Bologna, during which Louis XVIII. was permitted to assume his nephew's crown.

CHAPTER XX.

All this he related with an air of remarkable frankness and truth. Although not justified in believing him, I nevertheless was astonished at his knowledge of the most minute facts connected with the revolution. He spoke with much natural fluency, and his conversation abounded with a variety of curious anecdotes. There was something also of the soldier in his expression, without showing any want of that sort of elegance resulting from an intercourse with the best society.

"Will it be permitted me," I inquired, "to converse with you on equal terms, without making use of any titles?"

"That is what I myself wish you to do," was the reply. "I have at least reaped one advantage from adversity; I have learnt to smile at all these vanities. I assure you that I value myself more upon being a man, than having been born a prince."

We were in the habit of conversing together both night and morning, for a considerable time; and, in spite of what I considered the comic part of his character, he appeared to be of a good disposition, frank, affable, and interested in the virtue and happiness of mankind. More than once I was on the point of saying, "Pardon me; I wish I could believe you were Louis XVII., but I frankly confess I cannot prevail on myself to believe it; be equally sincere, I entreat you, and renounce this singular fiction of yours." I had even prepared to introduce the subject with an edifying discourse upon the vanity of all imposture, even of such untruths as may appear in themselves harmless.

I put off my purpose from day to day; I partly expected that we should grow still more friendly and confidential, but I had never the heart really to try the experiment upon his feelings. When I reflect upon this want of resolution, I sometimes attempt to reconcile myself to it on the ground of proper urbanity, unwillingness to give offence, and other reasons of the kind. Still these excuses are far from satisfying me; I cannot disguise that I ought not to have permitted my dislike to preaching him a sermon to stand in the way of speaking my real sentiments. To affect to give credit to imposture of any kind is miserable weakness, such as I think I should not, even in similar circumstances, exhibit again. At the same time, it must be confessed that, preface it as you will, it is a *harsh* thing to say to any one, "I don't believe you!" He will naturally resent it; it would deprive us of his friendship or regard: nay it would, perhaps, make him hate us. Yet it is better to run every risk than to sanction an untruth. Possibly, the man capable of it, upon finding that his imposture is known, will himself admire our sincerity, and afterwards be induced to reflect in a manner that may produce the best results.

The under-jailers were unanimously of opinion that he was really Louis XVII., and having already seen so many strange changes of fortune, they were not without hopes that he would some day ascend the throne of France, and remember the good treatment and attentions he had met with. With the exception of assisting in his escape, they made it their object to comply with all his wishes. It was by such means I had the honour of forming an acquaintance with this grand personage. He was of the middle height, between forty and forty-five years of age, rather inclined to corpulency, and had features strikingly like those of the Bourbons. It is very probable that this accidental resemblance may have led him to assume the character he did, and play so melancholy a part in it.

CHAPTER XXI.

There is one other instance of unworthy deference to private opinion, of which I must accuse myself. My neighbour was not an Atheist, he rather liked to converse on religious topics, as if he justly appreciated the importance of the subject, and was no stranger to its discussion. Still, he indulged a number of unreasonable prejudices against Christianity, which he regarded less in its real nature than its abuses. The superficial philosophy which preceded the French revolution had dazzled him. He had formed an idea that religious worship might be offered up with greater purity than as it had been dictated by the religion of the Evangelists. Without any intimate acquaintance with the writings of Condillac and Tracy, he venerated them as the most profound thinkers, and really thought that the last had carried the branch of metaphysics to the highest degree of perfection.

I may fairly say that *my* philosophical studies had been better directed; I was aware of the weakness of the experimental doctrine, and I knew the gross and shameless errors in point of criticism, which influenced the age of Voltaire in libelling Christianity. I had also read Guénée, and other able exposers of such false criticism. I felt a conviction that, by no logical reasoning, could the being of a God be granted, and the Bible rejected, and I conceived it a vulgar degradation to fall in with the stream of antichristian opinions, and to want elevation of intellect to apprehend how the doctrine of Catholicism in its true character, is religiously simple and ennobling. Yet I had the meanness to bow to human opinion out of deference and respect. The wit and sarcasms of my neighbour seemed to confound me, while I could not disguise from myself that they were idle and empty as the air. I dissimulated, I hesitated to announce my own belief, reflecting how far it were seasonable thus to contradict my companion, and persuading myself that it would be useless, and that I was perfectly justified in remaining silent. What vile pusillanimity! why thus respect the presumptuous power of popular errors and opinions, resting upon no foundation. True it is that an ill-timed zeal is always indiscreet, and calculated to irritate rather than convert; but to avow with frankness and modesty what we regard as an important truth, to do it even when we have reason to conclude it will not be palatable, and to meet willingly any ridicule or sarcasm which may be launched against it; this I maintain to be an actual duty. A noble avowal of this kind, moreover, may always be made, without pretending to assume, uncalled for, anything of the missionary character.

It is, I repeat, a duty, not to keep back an important truth at any period; for though there may be little hope of itt being immediately acknowledged: it may tend to prepare the minds of others, and in due time, doubtless, produce a better and more impartial judgment, and a consequent triumph of truth.

CHAPTER XXII.

I CONTINUED in the same apartment during a month and some days. On the night of February the 18th, 1821, I was roused from sleep by a loud noise of chains and keys; several men entered with a lantern, and the first idea that struck me was, that they were come to cut my throat.

While gazing at them in strange perplexity, one of the figures advanced towards me with a polite air; it was Count B——,* who requested I would dress myself as speedily as possible to set out.

I was surprised at this announcement, and even indulged a hope that they were sent to conduct me to the confines of Piedmont. Was it likely the storm which hung over me would thus early be dispersed? should I again enjoy that liberty so dearly prized, be restored to my beloved parents, and see my brothers and sisters?

I was allowed short time to indulge these flattering hopes. The moment I had thrown on my clothes, I followed my conductors without having an opportunity of bidding farewell to my royal neighbour. Yet I thought I heard him call my name, and regretted it was out of my power to stop and reply. "Where are we going?" I inquired of the Count, as we got into a coach, attended by an officer of the guard. "I cannot inform you till we shall be a mile on the other side the city of Milan." I was aware the coach was not going in the direction of the Vercelline gate; and my hopes suddenly vanished. I was silent; it was a beautiful moonlight night; I beheld the same well-known paths I had traversed for pleasure so many years before. The houses, the churches, and every object renewed a thousand pleasing recollections. I saw the *Corsia* of Porta Orientale, I saw the public gardens, where I had so often rambled with Foscolo,† Monti,‡ Lodovico di

* The Count Bolza, of the lake of Como, who has continued for years in the service of the Austrian Government, showing inexorable zeal in the capacity of a Commissary of Police.

† The learning of Ugo Foscolo, and the reputation he acquired by his *Hymn upon the Tombs*, his *Last Letters of Jacopo Ortis*, his *Treatises* upon Dante, Petrarch, Boccaccio, &c., are well-known in this country, where he spent a considerable portion of his life, and died in the year 1827.

‡ The Cavalier Vincenzo Monti stands at the head of the modern

Breme,* Pietro Borsieri,† Count Porro, and his sons, with many other delightful companions, conversing in all the glow of life and hope. How I felt my friendship for these noble men revive with double force when I thought of having parted from them for the last time, disappearing as they had done, one by one, so rapidly from my view. When we had gone a little way beyond the gate, I pulled my hat over my eyes, and indulged these sad retrospections unobserved.

After having gone about a mile, I addressed myself to Count B——. "I presume we are on the road to Verona." "Yes, further," was the reply; "we are for Venice, where it is my duty to hand you over to a special commission there appointed."

We travelled post, stopped nowhere, and on the 20th of February arrived at my destination. The September of the year preceding, just one month previous to my arrest, I had been at Venice, and had met a large and delightful party at dinner, in the Hotel della Luna. Strangely enough, I was now conducted by the Count and the officer to the very inn where we had spent that evening in social mirth.

One of the waiters started on seeing me, perceiving that,

poets of Italy. His stanzas on the *Death of Ugo Basville* obtained for him the title of *Dante Redivivo*. His works, both in verse and prose, are numerous, and generally acknowledged to be noble models in their several styles. His tragedy of *Aristodemo*, takes the lead among the most admirable specimens of the Italian drama. He died at Milan in the year 1829.

* Monsignor Lodovico di Breme, son of the Marquis of the same name, a Piedmontese, an intimate friend of the celebrated Madame de Staël, of Mons. Sismondi, &c., and a man of elevated sentiments, brilliant spirit, high cultivation, and accomplishments.

† Don Pietro Borsieri, son of a judge of the Court of Appeal at Milan, of which, previous to his receiving sentence of death, he was one of the state secretaries. He is the author of several little works and literary essays, all written with singular energy and chasteness of language.

though my conductors had assumed the dress of domestics, I was no other than a prisoner in their hands. I was gratified at this recognition, being persuaded that the man would mention my arrival there to more than one.

We dined, and I was then conducted to the palace of the Doge, where the tribunals are now held. I passed under the well-known porticoes of the *Procuratie*, and by the Florian Hotel, where I had enjoyed so many pleasant evenings the last autumn; but I did not happen to meet a single acquaintance. We went across the piazzetta, and there it struck me that the September before, I had met a poor mendicant, who addressed me in these singular words:—

"I see, sir, you are a stranger, but I cannot make out why you, sir, and all other strangers, should so much admire this place. To me it is a place of misfortune, and I never pass it when I can avoid it."

"What, did you here meet with some disaster?"

"I did, sir; a horrible one, sir; and not only I. God protect you from it, God protect you!" And he took himself off in haste.

At this moment it was impossible for me to forget the words of the poor beggarman. He was present there, too, the next year, when I ascended the scaffold, whence I heard read to me the sentence of death, and that it had been commuted for fifteen years hard imprisonment. Assuredly, if I had been inclined ever so little to superstition, I should have thought much of the mendicant, predicting to me with so much energy, as he did, and insisting that this was a place of misfortune. As it is, I have merely noted it down for a curious incident. We ascended the palace; Count B—— spoke to the judges, then, handing me over to the jailer, after embracing me with much emotion, he bade me farewell.

CHAPTER XXIII.

I FOLLOWED the jailer in silence. After turning through a number of passages, and several large rooms, we arrived at a small staircase, which brought us under the *Piombi*, those notorious state prisons, dating from the time of the Venetian republic.

There the jailer first registered my name, and then locked me up in the room appointed for me. The chambers called *I Piombi* consist of the upper portion of the Doge's palace, and are covered throughout with lead.

My room had a large window with enormous bars, and commanded a view of the roof (also of lead), and the church, of St. Mark. Beyond the church I could discern the end of the Piazza in the distance, with an immense number of cupolas and belfries on all sides. St. Mark's gigantic *Campanile* was separated from me only by the length of the church, and I could hear persons speaking from the top of it when they talked at all loud. To the left of the church was to be seen a portion of the grand court of the palace, and one of the chief entrances. There is a public well in that part of the court, and people were continually in the habit of going thither to draw water. From the lofty site of my prison they appeared to me about the size of little children, and I could not at all hear their conversation, except when they called out very loud. Indeed, I found myself much more solitary than I had been in the Milanese prisons.

During several days the anxiety I suffered from the criminal trial appointed by the special commission, made me rather melancholy, and it was increased, doubtless, by that painful feeling of deeper solitude.

I was here, moreover, further removed from my family, of whom I heard no more. The new faces that appeared wore a gloom at once strange and appalling. Report had greatly exaggerated the struggle of the Milanese and the rest of Italy to recover their independence; it was doubted if I were not one of the most desperate promoters of that mad enterprise. I found that my name, as a writer, was not wholly unknown to my jailer, to his wife, and even his daughter, besides two sons, and the under-jailers, all of whom, by their manner, seemed to have an idea that a writer of tragedies was little better than a kind of magician. They looked grave and distant, yet as if eager to learn more of me, had they dared to waive the ceremony of their iron office.

In a few days I grew accustomed to their looks, or rather, I think, they found I was not so great a necromancer as to escape through the lead roofs, and, consequently, assumed a more conciliating demeanour. The wife had most of the character that marks the true jailer; she was dry and hard, all bone, without a particle of heart, about forty, and incapable of feeling, except it were a savage sort of instinct for her offspring. She used to bring me my coffee, morning and afternoon, and my water at dinner. She was generally accompanied by her daughter, a girl of about fifteen, not very pretty, but with mild, compassionating looks, and her two sons, from ten to thirteen years of age. They always went back with their mother, but there was a gentle look and a smile of love for me upon their young faces as she closed the door, my only company when they were gone. The jailer never came near me, except to conduct me before the special commission, that terrible ordeal for what are termed crimes of state.

The under-jailers, occupied with the prisons of the police, situated on a lower floor, where there were numbers of robbers, seldom came near me. One of these assistants was an old man, more than seventy, but still able to discharge his laborious duties, and to run up and down the steps to the different prisons; another was a young man about twenty-five, more bent upon giving an account of his love affairs than eager to devote himself to his office.

CHAPTER XXIV.

I HAD now to confront the terrors of a state trial. What was my dread of implicating others by my answers! What difficulty to contend against so many strange accusations, so many suspicions of all kinds! How impossible, almost, not to become implicated by these incessant examinations, by daily new arrests, and the imprudence of other parties, perhaps not known to you, yet belonging to the same movement! I have decided not to speak on politics; and I must suppress every detail connected with the state trials. I shall merely observe that, after being subjected for successive hours to the harassing process, I retired in a frame of mind so excited, and so enraged, that I should assuredly have taken my own life, had not the voice of religion, and the recollection of my parents restrained my hand. I lost the tranquillity of mind I had acquired at Milan; during many days, I despaired of regaining it, and I cannot even allude to this interval without feelings of horror. It was vain to attempt it, I could not pray; I questioned the justice of God; I cursed mankind, and all the world, revolving in my mind all the possible sophisms and satires I could think of, respecting the hollowness and vanity of virtue. The disappointed and the exasperated are always ingenious in finding accusations against their fellow-creatures, and even the Creator himself. Anger is of a more universal and injurious tendency than is generally supposed. As we cannot rage and storm from morning till night, and as the most ferocious animal has necessarily its intervals of repose, these intervals in man are greatly influenced by the immoral character of the conduct which may have preceded them. He appears to be at peace, indeed, but it is an irreligious, malignant peace; a savage sardonic smile, destitute of all charity or dignity; a love of confusion, intoxication, and sarcasm.

In this state I was accustomed to sing—anything but hymns—with a kind of mad, ferocious joy. I spoke to all who approached my dungeon, jeering and bitter things; and I tried to look upon the whole creation through the medium of that commonplace wisdom, the wisdom of the cynics. This degrading period, on which I hate to reflect, lasted happily only for six or seven days, during which my Bible had become covered with dust. One of the jailer's boys, thinking to please me, as he cast his eye upon it, observed, "Since you left off reading that great, ugly book, you don't seem half so melancholy, sir." "Do you think so?" said I. Taking the Bible in my hands, I wiped off the dust, and opening it hastily, my eyes fell upon the following words:—"And he said unto his disciples, it must needs be that offences come; but woe unto him by whom they come; for better had it been for him that a millstone were hanged about his neck, and he cast into the sea, than that he should offend one of these little ones."

I was affected upon reading this passage, and I felt ashamed when I thought that this little boy had perceived, from the dust with which it was covered, that I no longer read my Bible, and had even supposed that I had acquired a better temper by want of attention to my religious duties, and become less wretched by forgetting my God. "You little graceless fellow," I exclaimed, though reproaching him in a gentle tone, and grieved at having afforded him a subject of scandal; "this is not a great, ugly book, and for the few days that I have left off reading it, I find myself much worse. If your mother would let you stay with me a little while, you would see that I know how to get rid of my ill-humour. If you knew how hard it was to be in good humour, when left so long alone, and when you hear me singing and talking like a madman, you would not call this a great ugly book."

CHAPTER XXV.

The boy left me, and I felt a sort of pleasure at having taken the Bible again in my hands, more especially at having owned I had been worse for having neglected it. It seemed as if I had made atonement to a generous friend whom I had unjustly offended, but had now become reconciled to. Yes! I had even forgotten my God! I exclaimed, and perverted my better nature. Could I have been led to believe that the vile mockery of the cynic was applicable to one in my forlorn and desperate situation?

I felt an indescribable emotion on asking myself this question; I placed the Bible upon a chair, and, falling on my knees, I burst into tears of remorse: I who ever found it so difficult to shed even a tear. These tears were far more delightful to me than any physical enjoyment I had ever felt. I felt I was restored to God, I loved him, I repented of having outraged religion by degrading myself: and I made a vow never, never more to forget, to separate myself from, my God.

How truly a sincere return to faith, and love, and hope, consoles and elevates the mind. I read and continued to weep for upwards of an hour. I rose with renewed confidence that God had not abandoned me, but had forgiven my every fault and folly. It was then that my misfortunes, the horrors of my continued examinations, and the probable death which awaited me, appeared of little account. I rejoiced in suffering, since I was thus afforded an occasion to perform some duty, and that, by submitting with a resigned mind, I was obeying my Divine Master. I was enabled, thanks be to Heaven, to read my Bible. I no longer estimated it by the wretched, critical subterfuges of a Voltaire, heaping ridicule upon mere expressions, in themselves neither false nor ridiculous, except to gross ignorance or malice, which cannot penetrate their meaning. I became clearly convinced how indisputably it was the code of sanctity, and hence of truth itself; how really unphilosophical it was to take offence at a few little imperfections of style, not less absurd than the vanity of one who despises everything that wears not the gloss of elegant forms; what still greater absurdity to imagine that such a collection of books, so long held in religious veneration, should not possess an authentic origin, boasting, as they do, such a vast superiority over the Koran, and the old theology of the Indies.

Many, doubtless, abused its excellence, many wished to turn it into a code of injustice, and a sanction of all their bad passions. But the triumphant answer to these is, that every thing is liable to abuse; and when did the abuse of the most precious and best of things lead us to the conclusion that they were in their own nature bad? Our Saviour himself declared it; the whole law and the Prophets, the entire body of these sacred books, all inculcate the same precept to love God and mankind. And must not such writings embrace the truth—truth adapted to all times and ages? must they not ever constitute the living word of the Holy Spirit?

Whilst I made these reflections, I renewed my intention of identifying with religion all my thoughts concerning human affairs, all my opinions upon the progress of civilisation, my philanthropy, love of my country, in short, all the passions of my mind.

The few days in which I remained subjected to the cynic doctrine, did me a deal of harm. I long felt its effects, and had great difficulty to remove them. Whenever man yields in the least to the temptation of undignifying his intellect, to view the works of

God through the infernal medium of scorn, to abandon the beneficent exercise of prayer, the injury which he inflicts upon his natural reason prepares him to fall again with but little struggle. For a period of several weeks I was almost daily assaulted with strong, bitter tendencies to doubt and disbelief; and it called for the whole power of my mind to free myself from their grasp.

CHAPTER XXVI.

When these mental struggles had ceased, and I had again become habituated to reverence the Deity in all my thoughts and feelings, I for some time enjoyed the most unbroken serenity and peace. The examinations to which I was every two or three days subjected by the special commission, however tormenting, produced no lasting anxiety, as before. I succeeded in this arduous position, in discharging all which integrity and friendship required of me, and left the rest to the will of God. I now, too, resumed my utmost efforts to guard against the effects of any sudden surprise, every emotion and passion, and every imaginable misfortune; a kind of preparation for future trials of the greatest utility.

My solitude, meantime, grew more oppressive. Two sons of the jailer, whom I had been in the habit of seeing at brief intervals, were sent to school; and I saw them no more. The mother and the sister, who had been accustomed, along with them, to speak to me, never came near me, except to bring my coffee. About the mother I cared very little; but the daughter, though rather plain, had something so pleasing and gentle, both in her words and looks, that I greatly felt the loss of them. Whenever she brought the coffee, and said, "It was I who made it," I always thought it excellent: but when she observed, "This is my mother's making," it lost all its relish.

Being almost deprived of human society, I one day made

acquaintance with some ants upon my window; I fed them; they went away, and ere long the placed was thronged with these little insects, as if come by invitation. A spider, too, had weaved a noble edifice upon my walls, and I often gave him a feast of gnats or flies, which were extremely annoying to me, and which he liked much better than I did. I got quite accustomed to the sight of him; he would run over my bed, and come and take the precious morsels out of my hand. Would to heaven these had been the only insects which visited my abode. It was still summer, and the gnats had begun to multiply to a prodigious and alarming extent. The previous winter had been remarkably mild, and after the prevalence of the March winds followed extreme heat. It is impossible to convey an idea of the insufferable oppression of the air in the place I occupied. Opposed directly to a noontide sun, under a leaden roof, and with a window looking on the roof of St. Mark, casting a tremendous reflection of the heat, I was nearly suffocated. I had never conceived an idea of a punishment so intolerable: add to which the clouds of gnats, which, spite of my utmost efforts, covered every article of furniture in the room, till even the walls and ceiling seemed alive with them; and I had some apprehension of being devoured alive. Their bites, moreover, were extremely painful, and when thus punctured from morning till night, only to undergo the same operation from day to day, and engaged the whole time in killing and slaying, some idea may be formed of the state both of my body and my mind.

I felt the full force of such a scourge, yet was unable to obtain a change of dungeon, till at length I was tempted to rid myself of my life, and had strong fears of running distracted. But, thanks be to God, these thoughts were not of long duration, and religion continued to sustain me. It taught me that man was born to suffer, and to suffer with courage: it taught me to experience a sort of pleasure in my troubles, to resist and to vanquish in the battle appointed me by Heaven. The more unhappy, I said to myself, my life may become, the less will I yield to my fate, even though I should be condemned in the morning of my life to the scaffold. Perhaps, without these preliminary and chastening trials, I might have met death in an unworthy manner. Do I know, moreover, that I possess those virtues and qualities which deserve prosperity; where and what are they? Then, seriously examining into my past conduct, I found too little good on which to pride myself; the chief part was a tissue of vanity, idolatry, and the mere exterior of virtue. Unworthy, therefore, as I am, let me suffer! If it be intended that men and gnats should destroy me, unjustly or otherwise, acknowledge in them the instruments of a divine justice, and be silent.

CHAPTER XXVII.

Does man stand in need of compulsion before he can be brought to humble himself with sincerity? to look upon himself as a sinner? Is it not too true that we in general dissipate our youth in vanity, and, instead of employing all our faculties in the acquisition of what is good, make them the instruments of our degradation? There are, doubtless, exceptions, but I confess they cannot apply to a wretched individual like myself. There is no merit in thus being dissatisfied with myself; when we see a lamp which emits more smoke than flame, it requires no great sincerity to say that it does not burn as it ought to do.

Yes, without any degradation, without any scruples of hypocrisy, and viewing myself with perfect tranquillity of mind, I perceived that I had merited the chastisement of my God. An internal monitor told me that such chastisements were, for one fault or other, amply merited; they assisted in winning me back to Him who is perfect, and whom every human being, as far as their limited powers will admit, are bound to imitate. By what right, while constrained to condemn myself for innumerable offences and forgetfulness towards God, could I complain, because some men appeared to me despicable, and others wicked? What if I were deprived of all worldly advantages, and was doomed to linger in prison, or to die a violent death? I sought to impress upon my mind reflections like these, at once just and applicable; and this done, I found it was necessary to be consistent, and that it could be effected in no other manner than by sanctifying the upright judgments of the Almighty, by loving them, and eradicating every wish at all opposed to them. The better to persevere in my intention, I determined, in future, carefully to revolve in my mind all my opinions, by committing them to writing. The difficulty was that the commission, while permitting me to have the use of ink and paper, counted out the leaves, with an express prohibition that I should not destroy a single one, and reserving the power of examining in what manner I had employed them. To supply the want of paper, I had recourse to the simple stratagem of smoothing with a piece of glass a rude table which I had, and upon this I daily wrote my long meditations respecting the duties of mankind, and especially of those which applied to myself. It is no exaggeration to say that the hours so employed were sometimes delightful to me, notwithstanding the difficulty of breathing I experienced from the excessive heat, to say nothing of the bitterly painful wounds, small though they were, of those poisonous gnats. To defend myself from the countless numbers of these tormentors, I was compelled, in the midst of suffocation, to wrap my head and my legs in thick cloth, and not only write with gloves on, but to bandage my wrist to prevent the intruders creeping up my sleeves.

Meditations like mine assumed somewhat of a biographical character. I made out an account of all the good and the evil which had grown up with me from my earliest youth, discussing them within myself, attempting to resolve every doubt, and arranging, to the best of my power, the various kinds of knowledge I had acquired, and my ideas upon every subject. When the whole surface of the table was covered with my lucubrations, I perused and re-perused them, meditated on what I had already meditated, and, at length, resolved (however unwillingly) to scratch out all I had done with the glass, in order to have a clean superficies upon which to recommence my operations.

From that time I continued the narrative of my experience of good and evil, always relieved by digressions of every kind, by some analysis of this or that point, whether in metaphysics, morals, politics, or religion; and when the whole was complete, I again began to read, and re-read, and lastly, to scratch out. Being anxious to avoid every chance of interruption, or of impediment, to my repeating with the greatest possible freedom the facts I had recorded, and my opinions upon them, I took care to transpose and abbreviate the words in such a manner as to run no risk from the most inquisitorial visit. No search, however, was made, and no one was aware that I was spending my miserable prison-hours to so good a purpose. Whenever I heard the jailer or other person open the door I covered my little table with a cloth, and placed upon it the ink-stand, with the *lawful* quantity of state paper by its side.

CHAPTER XXVIII.

STILL I did not wholly neglect the paper put into my hands, and sometimes even devoted an entire day or night to writing. But here I only treated of literary matters. I composed at that time the *Ester d'Engaddi*, the *Iginia d'Asti*, and the *Cantichi*, entitled, *Tancreda Rosilde*, *Eligi* and *Valafrido*, *Adello*, besides several sketches of tragedies, and other productions, in the list of which was a poem upon the *Lombard League*, and another upon *Christopher Columbus*.

As it was not always so easy an affair to get a reinforcement of paper, I was in the habit of committing my rough draughts to my table, or the wrapping-paper in which I received fruit and other articles. At times I would give away my dinner to the under-jailer, telling him that I had no appetite, and then requesting from him the favour of a sheet of paper. This was, however, only in certain exigencies, when my little table was full of writing, and I had not yet determined on clearing it away. I was often very hungry, and though the jailer had money of mine in his possession, I did not ask him to bring me anything to eat, partly lest he should suspect I had given away my dinner, and partly that the under-jailer might not find out that I had said the thing which was not when I assured him of my loss of appetite. In the evening I regaled myself with some strong coffee, and I entreated that it might be made by the little *sioa*, Zanze.* This was the jailer's daughter, who, if she could escape the lynx-eye of her sour mamma, was good enough to make it exceedingly good; so good, indeed, that, what with the emptiness of my stomach, it produced a kind of convulsion, which kept me awake the whole of the night.

In this state of gentle inebriation, I felt my intellectual faculties strangely invigorated; wrote poetry, philosophized, and prayed till morning with feelings of real pleasure. I then became completely exhausted, threw myself upon my bed, and, spite of the gnats that were continually sucking my blood, I slept an hour or two in profound rest.

* La Signora Angiola.

I can hardly describe the peculiar and pleasing exaltation of mind which continued for nights together, and I left no means untried to secure the same means of continuing it. With this view I still refused to touch a mouthful of dinner, even when I was in no want of paper, merely in order to obtain my magic beverage for the evening.

How fortunate I thought myself when I succeeded; not unfrequently the coffee was not made by the gentle Angiola; and it was always vile stuff from her mother's hands. In this last case, I was sadly put out of humour, for instead of the electrical effect on my nerves, it made me wretched, weak, and hungry; I threw myself down to sleep, but was unable to close an eye. Upon these occasions I complained bitterly to Angiola, the jailer's daughter, and one day, as if she had been in fault, I scolded her so sharply that the poor girl began to weep, sobbing out, "Indeed, sir, I never deceived anybody, and yet everybody calls me a deceitful little minx."

"Everybody! Oh then, I see I am not the only one driven to distraction by your vile slops."

"I do not mean to say that, sir. Ah, if you only knew; if I dared to tell you all that my poor, wretched heart——"

"Well, don't cry so! What is all this ado? I beg your pardon, you see, if I scolded you. Indeed, I believe you would not, you could not, make me such vile stuff as this."

"Dear me! I am not crying about that, sir."

"You are not!" and I felt my self-love not a little mortified, though I forced a smile. "Are you crying, then, because I scolded you, and yet not about the coffee?"

"Yes, indeed, sir?"

"Ah! then who called you a little deceitful one before?"

"*He* did, sir."

"*He* did; and who is *he?*"

"My lover, sir;" and she hid her face in her little hands.

Afterwards she ingenuously intrusted to my keeping, and I could not well betray her, a little serio-comic sort of pastoral romance, which really interested me.

CHAPTER XXIX.

FROM that day forth, I know not why, I became the adviser and confidant of this young girl, who returned and conversed with me for hours. She at first said, "You are so good, sir, that I feel just the same when I am here as if I were your own daughter."

"That is a very poor compliment," replied I, dropping her hand; "I am hardly yet thirty-two, and you look upon me as if I were an old father."

"No, no, not so; I mean as a brother, to be sure;" and she insisted upon taking hold of my hand with an air of the most innocent confidence and affection.

I am glad, thought I to myself, that you are no beauty; else, alas, this innocent sort of fooling might chance to disconcert me; at other times I thought it is lucky, too, she is so young, there could never be any danger of becoming attached to girls of her years. At other times, however, I felt a little uneasy, thinking I was mistaken in having pronounced her rather plain, whereas her whole shape and features were by no means wanting in proportion or expression. If she were not quite so pale, I said, and her face free from those marks, she might really pass for a beauty. It is impossible, in fact, not to find some charm in the presence and in the looks and voice of a young girl full of vivacity and affection. I had taken not the least pains to acquire her good-will; yet was I as dear to either the as a father or a brother, whichever title I preferred. And why? Only because she had read *Francesca da Rimini* and *Eufemio*, and my poems, she said, had made her weep so often; then, besides, I was a solitary prisoner, *without having*, as she observed, either robbed or murdered anybody.

In short, when I had become attached to poor Maddalene, without once seeing her, how was it likely that I could remain indifferent to the sisterly assiduity and attentions, to the thousand pleasing little compliments, and to the most delicious cups of coffee of this young Venice girl, my gentle little jailer?* I should be trying to impose on myself, were I to attribute to my own prudence the fact of my not having fallen in love with Angiola. I did not do so, simply from the circumstance of her having already a lover of her own choosing, to whom she was desperately, unalterably attached. Heaven help me! if it had not been thus I should have found myself in a very *critical* position, indeed, for an author, with so little to keep alive his attention. The sentiment I felt for her was not, then, what is called love. I wished to see her happy, and that she might be united to the lover of her choice; I was not jealous, nor had I the remotest idea she could ever select me as the object of her regard. Still, when I heard my prison-door open, my heart began to beat in the hope it was my Angiola; and if she appeared not, I experienced a peculiar kind of vexation; when she really came my heart throbbed yet more violently, from a feeling of pure joy. Her parents, who had begun to entertain a good opinion of me, and were aware of her passionate regard for another, offered no opposition to the visits she thus made me, permitting her almost invariably to bring me my coffee in a morning, and not unfrequently in the evening.

There was altogether a simplicity and an affectionateness in her every word, look, and gesture, which were really captivating. She would say, "I am excessively attached to another, and yet I take such delight in being near you!

* "Venezianina adolescente sbirra?"

When I am not in *his* company, I like being nowhere so well as here." (Here was another compliment.)

"And don't you know why?" inquired I.

"I do not."

"I will tell you, then. It is because I permit you to talk about your lover."

"That is a good guess; yet still I think it is a good deal because I esteem you so very much!"

Poor girl! along with this pretty frankness she had that blessed sin of taking me always by the hand, and pressing it with all her heart, not perceiving that she at once pleased and disconcerted me by her affectionate manner. Thanks be to Heaven, that I can always recall this excellent little girl to mind without the least tinge of remorse.

CHAPTER XXX.

The following portion of my narrative would assuredly have been more interesting had the gentle Angiola fallen in love with me, or if I had at least run half mad to enliven my solitude. There was, however, another sentiment, that of simple benevolence, no less dear to me, which united our hearts in one. And if, at any moment, I felt there was the least risk of its changing its nature in my vain, weak heart, it produced only sincere regret.

Once, certainly, having my doubts that this would happen, and finding her, to my sorrow, a hundred times more beautiful than I had at first imagined; feeling too so very melancholy when she was absent, so joyous when near, I took upon myself to play the *unamiable*, in the idea that this would remove all danger by making her leave off the same affectionate and familiar manner. This innocent stratagem was tried in vain; the poor girl was so patient, so full of compassion for me. She would look at me in silence, with her elbow resting upon the window, and say, after a long pause, "I see, sir, you are tired of my company, yet *I* would stay here the whole day if I could, merely to keep the hours from hanging so heavy upon you. This ill-humour of yours is the natural effect of your long solitude; if you were able to chat awhile, you would be quite well again. If you don't like to talk, I will talk for you."

"About your lover, eh?"

"No, no; not always about him; I can talk of many things."

She then began to give me some extracts from the household annals, dwelling upon the sharp temper of her mother, her good-natured father, and the monkey-tricks of her little brothers; and she told all this with a simple grace and innocent frankness not a little alluring. Yet I was pretty near the truth; for, without being aware of it, she uniformly concluded with the one favourite theme: her ill-starred love. Still I went on acting the part of the *unamiable*, in the hope that she would take a spite against me. But whether from inadvertency or design, she would not take the hint, and I was at last fairly compelled to give up by sitting down contented to let her have her way, smiling, sympathising with, and thanking her for the sweet patience with which she had so long borne with me.

I no longer indulged the ungracious idea of spiting her against me, and, by degrees, all my other fears were allayed. Assuredly I had not been smitten; I long examined into the nature of my scruples, wrote down my reflections upon the subject, and derived no little advantage from the process.

Man often terrifies himself with mere bugbears of the mind. If we would learn not to fear them, we have only to examine them a little more nearly and attentively. What harm, then, if I looked forward to her visits to me with a tender anxiety, if I appreciated their sweetness, if it did me good to be compassioned by her, and to interchange all our thoughts and feelings, unsullied, I will say, as those of childhood. Even her most affectionate looks, and smiles, and pressures of the hand, while they agitated me, produced a feeling of salutary respect mingled with compassion. One evening, I remember, when suffering under a sad misfortune, the poor girl threw her arms round my neck, and wept as if her heart would break. She had not the least idea of impropriety; no daughter could embrace a father with more perfect innocence and unsuspecting affection.' I could not, however, reflect upon that embrace without feeling somewhat agitated. It often recurred to my imagination, and I could then think of no other subject. On another occasion, when she thus threw herself upon my confidence, I was really obliged to disentangle myself from her dear arms, ere I once pressed her to my bosom, or gave her a single kiss, while I stammered out, "I pray you, now, sweet Angiola, do not embrace me ever again; it is not quite proper." She fixed her eyes upon me for a moment, then cast them down, while a blush suffused her ingenuous countenance; and I am sure it was the first time that she read in my mind even the possibility of any weakness of mine in reference to her. Still she did not cease to continue her visits upon the same friendly footing, with a little more reserve and respect, such as I wished it to be; and I was grateful to her for it.

CHAPTER XXXI.

I AM unable to form an estimate of the evils which afflict others; but, as respects myself, I am bound to confess that, after close examination, I found that no sufferings had been appointed me, except to some wise end, and for my own advantage. It was thus even with the excessive heat which oppressed, and the gnats which tormented me. Often have I reflected that but for this continual suffering I might not have successfully resisted the temptation of falling in love, situated as I was, and with one whose extremely affectionate and ardent feelings would have made it difficult always to preserve it within respectful limits. If I had sometimes reason to tremble, how should I have been enabled to regulate my vain imagination in an atmosphere somewhat inspiring, and open to the breathings of joy.

Considering the imprudence of Angiola's parents, who reposed such confidence in me, the imprudence of the poor girl herself, who had not an idea of giving rise to any culpable affection on my part, and considering, too, the little steadfastness of my virtue, there can be little doubt but the suffocating heat of my great oven, and the cruel warfare of the gnats, were effectual safeguards to us both.

Such a reflection reconciled me somewhat to these scourges; and I then asked myself, Would you consent to become free, and to take possession of some handsome apartment, filled with flowers and fresh air, on condition of never more seeing this affectionate being? I will own the truth; I had not courage to reply to this simple question.

When you really feel interested about any one, it is indescribable what mere trifles are capable of conferring pleasure. A single word, a smile, a tear, a Venetian turn of expression, her eagerness in protecting me from my enemies, the gnats, all inspired me with a childish delight that lasted the whole day. What most gratified me was to see that her own sufferings seemed to be relieved by conversing with me, that my compassion consoled her, that my advice influenced her, and that her heart was susceptible of the warmest devotion when treating of virtue and its great Author.

When we had sometimes discussed the subject of religion, she would observe, "I find that I can now pray with more willingness and more faith than I did." At other times, suddenly breaking off some frivolous topic, she took the Bible, opened it, pressed her lips to it, and then begged of me to translate some passages, and give my comments. She added, "I could wish that every time you happen to recur to this passage you should call to mind that I have kissed and kissed it again."

It was not always, indeed, that her kisses fell so appropriately, more especially if she happened to open at the spiritual songs. Then, in order to spare her blushes, I took advantage of her want of acquaintance with the Latin, and gave a turn to the expressions which, without detracting from the sacredness of tho Bible, might serve to respect her innocence. On such occasions I never once permitted myself to smile; at the same time I was not a little perplexed, when, not rightly comprehending my new version, she entreated of me to translate the whole, word for word, and would by no means let me shy the question by turning her attention to something else.

CHAPTER XXXII.

NOTHING is durable here below! Poor Angiola fell sick; and on one of the first days when she felt indisposed, she came to see me, complaining bitterly of pains in her head. She wept, too, and would not explain the cause of her grief. She only murmured something that looked like reproaches of her lover. "He is a villain!" she said; "but God forgive him, as I do!"

I left no means untried to obtain her confidence, but it was the first time I was quite unable to ascertain why she distressed herself to such an excess. "I will return tomorrow morning," she said, one evening on parting from me; "I will, indeed." But the next morning came, and my coffee was brought by her mother; the next, and tho next, by the under-jailers; and Angiola continued griovously ill. The under-jailers, also, brought me very unpleasant tidings relating to the love-affair; tidings, in short, which made me deeply sympathize with her sufferings. A case of seduction! But, perhaps, it was the tale of calumny. Alas! I but too well believed it, and I was affected at it more than I can express; though I still like to flatter myself that it was false. After upwards of a month's illness, the poor girl was taken into the country, and I saw her no more.

It is astonishing how deeply I felt this deprivation, and how much more horrible my solitude now appeared. Still more bitter was the reflection that she, who had so tenderly fed, and watched, and visited me in my sad prison, supplying every want and wish within her power, was herself a prey to sorrow and misfortune. Alas! I could make her no return; yet, surely she will feel aware how truly I sympathize with her; that there is no effort I would not make to afford her comfort and relief, and that I shall never cease to offer up my prayers for her, and to bless her for her goodness to a wretched prisoner.

Though her visits had been too brief, they were enough to break upon the horrid monotony of my solitude. By suggesting and comparing our ideas, I obtained new views and feelings, exercised some of tho best and sweetest affections, gave a zest to life, and even threw a sort of lustre round my misfortunes.

Suddenly the vision fled, and my dungeon became to me really like a living tomb. A strange sadness for many days quite oppressed me. I could not even write: it was a dark, quiet, nameless feeling, in no way partaking of the violence and irritation which I had before experienced. Was it that I had become more inured to adversity, more philosophical, more of a Christian? Or was it really that the extremely enervating heat of my dungeon had so prostrated my powers that I could no longer feel the pangs of excessive grief. Ah, no! for I can well recollect that I then felt it to my inmost soul; and, perhaps, more intensely from the want both of will and power to give vent to it by agitation, maledictions, and cries. The fact is, I believe, that I had been severely schooled by my past sufferings, and was resigned to the will of God. I had so often maintained that it was a mark of cowardice to complain, that, at length, I succeeded in restraining my passion, when on the point of breaking out, and felt vexed that I had permitted it to obtain any ascendancy over me.

My mental faculties were strengthened by the habit of writing down my thoughts; I got rid of all my vanity, and reduced the chief part of my reasonings to the following conclusions: There is a God: THEREFORE unerring justice; THEREFORE all that happens is ordained to the best end; consequently, the sufferings of man on earth are inflicted for the good of man.

Thus, my acquaintance with Angiola had proved beneficial, by soothing and conciliating my feelings. Her good opinion of me had urged me to the fulfilment of many duties, especially of that of proving one's self superior to the shocks of fortune, and of suffering in patience. By exerting myself to persevere for about a month, I was enabled to feel perfectly resigned.

Angiola had beheld me two or three times in a downright passion; once, as I have stated, on account of her having brought me bad coffee, and a second time as follows:—

Every two or three weeks the jailer had brought me a letter from some of my family. It was previously submitted to the Commission, and most roughly handled, as was too evident by the number of *erasures* in the blackest ink which appeared throughout. One day, however, instead of merely striking out a few passages, they drew the black line over the entire letter, with the exception of the words, "My Dearest Silvio," at the beginning, and the parting salutation at the close, "*All unite in kindest love to you.*"

This act threw me into such an uncontrollable fit of passion, that, in presence of the gentle Angiola, I broke out into violent shouts of rage, and cursed I know not whom. The poor girl pitied me from her heart; but, at the same time, reminded me of the strange inconsistency of my principles. I saw she had reason on her side, and I ceased from uttering my maledictions.

CHAPTER XXXIII.

One of the under-jailers one day entered my prison with a mysterious look, and said, "Sometime, I believe, that Siora Zanze (Angiola) . . . was used to bring you your coffee. . . . She stopped a good while to converse with you, and I was afraid the cunning one would worm out all your secrets, sir."

"Not one," I replied, in great anger; "or if I had any, I should not be such a fool as to tell them in that way. Go on."

"Beg pardon, sir; far from me to call you by such a name. . . . But I never trusted to that Siora Zanze. And now, sir, as you have no longer any one to keep you company. . . . I trust I ——"

"What, what! explain yourself at once!"

"Swear first that you will not betray me."

"Well, well; I could do that with a safe conscience. I never betrayed any one."

"Do you say really you will swear?"

"Yes; I swear not to betray you. But what a wretch to doubt it; for any one capable of betraying you will not scruple to violate an oath."

He took a letter from his coat-lining, and gave it me with

a trembling hand, beseeching I would destroy it the moment I had read it."

"Stop," I cried, opening it; "I will read and destroy it while you are here."

"But, sir, you must answer it, and I cannot stop now. Do it at your leisure. Only take heed, when you hear any one coming, you will know if it be I by my singing, pretty loudly, the tune, *Sognai mi gera un gato.* You need, then, fear nothing, and may keep the letter quietly in your pocket. But should you not hear this song, set it down for a mark that it cannot be me, or that some one is with me. Then, in a moment, out with it, don't trust to any concealment, in case of a search; out with it. tear it into a thousand bits, and throw it through the window."

"Depend upon me; I see you are prudent, I will be so too."

"Yet you called me a stupid wretch."

"You do right to reproach me," I replied, shaking him by the hand, "and I beg your pardon." He went away, and I began to read:—

"I am (and here followed the name) one of your admirers: I have all your *Francesca da Rimini* by heart. They arrested me for—(and here he gave the reason with the date) —and I would give, I know not how many pounds of my blood to have the pleasure of being with you, or at least in a dungeon near yours, in order that we might converse together. Since I heard from Tremerello, so we shall call our confidant, that you, sir, were a prisoner, and the cause of your arrest, I have longed to tell you how deeply I lament your misfortune, and that no one can feel greater attachment to you than myself. Have you any objection to accept the offer I make, namely, that we should try to lighten the burden of our solitude by writing to each other. I pledge you my honour, that not a being shall ever hear of our correspondence from me, and am persuaded that I may count upon the same secresy on your part, if you adopt my plan. Meantime, that you may form some idea, I will give you an abstract from my life."—(It followed.)

CHAPTER XXXIV.

The reader, however deficient in the imaginative organ, may easily conceive the electric effect of such a letter upon the nerves of a poor prisoner, not of the most savage disposition, but possessing an affectionate and gregarious turn of mind. I felt already an affection for the unknown; I pitied his misfortunes, and was grateful for the kind expressions he made use of. "Yes," exclaimed I, your generous purpose shall be effected. I wish my letters may afford you consolation equal to that which I shall derive from yours."

I re-perused his letter with almost boyish delight, and blessed the writer; there was not an expression which did not exhibit evidence of a clear and noble mind.

The sun was setting, it was my hour of prayer; I felt the presence of God; how sincere was my gratitude for his providing me with new means of exercising the faculties of my mind. How it revived my recollection of all the invaluable blessings he had bestowed upon me!

I stood before the window, with my arms between the bars, and my hands folded; the church of St. Mark lay below me, an immense flock of pigeons, free as the air, were flying about, were cooing and billing, or busied in constructing their nests upon the leaden roof; the heavens in their magnificence were before me; I surveyed all that part of Venice visible from my prison; a distant murmur of human voices broke sweetly on my ear. From this vast unhappy prison-house did I hold communion with Him, whose eyes alone behold me; to Him I recommended my father, my mother, and, individually, all those most dear to me, and it appeared as if I heard Him reply, "Confide in my goodness," and I exclaimed, "Thy goodness assures me."

I concluded my prayer with much emotion, greatly comforted, and little caring for the bites of the gnats, which had been joyfully feasting upon me. The same evening, my mind, after such exaltation, beginning to grow calmer, I found the torment from the gnats becoming insufferable, and while engaged in wrapping up my hands and face, a vulgar and malignant idea all at once entered my mind, which horrified me, and which I vainly attempted to banish.

Tremerello had insinuated a vile suspicion respecting Angiola; that, in short, she was a spy upon my secret opinions! She! that noble-hearted creature, who knew nothing of politics, and wished to know nothing of them!

It was impossible for me to suspect her; but have I, said I, the same certainty respecting Tremerello? Suppose that rogue should be the bribed instrument of secret informers; suppose the letter had been fabricated by *who knows whom*, to induce me to make important disclosures to my new friend. Perhaps his pretended prison does not exist; or if so, he may be a traitor, eager to worm out secrets in order to make his own terms; perhaps he is a man of honour, and Tremerello himself the traitor who aims at our destruction in order to gain an additional salary.

Oh, horrible thought, yet too natural to the unhappy prisoner, everywhere in fear of enmity and fraud!

Such suspicions tormented and degraded me. I did not entertain them as regarded Angiola a single moment. Yet, from what Tremerello had said, a kind of doubt clung to me as to the conduct of those who had permitted her to come into my apartment. Had they, either from their own zeal, or by superior authority, given her the office of spy? in that case, how ill had she discharged such an office!

But what was I to do respecting the letter of the unknown? Should I adopt the severe, repulsive counsel of fear which we call prudence? Shall I return the letter to Tremerello, and tell him, I do not wish to run any risk. Yet suppose there should be no treason; and the unknown be a truly worthy character, deserving that I should venture something, if only to relieve the horrors of his solitude? Coward as I am, standing on the brink of death, the fatal decree ready to strike me at any moment, yet to refuse to perform a simple act of love! Reply to him I must and will. Grant that it be discovered, no one can fairly be accused of writing the letter, though poor Tremerello would assuredly meet with the severest chastisement. Is not this consideration of itself sufficient to decide me against undertaking any clandestine correspondence? Is it not my absolute duty to decline it?

CHAPTER XXXV.

I WAS agitated the whole evening; I never closed my eyes that night, and amidst so many conflicting doubts, I knew not on what to resolve.

I sprung from my bed before dawn, I mounted upon the window-place, and offered up my prayers. In trying circumstances it is necessary to appeal with confidence to God, to heed his inspirations, and to adhere to them.

This I did, and after long prayer, I went down, shook off the gnats, took the bitten gloves in my hands, and came to the determination to explain my apprehensions to Tremerello and warn him of the great danger to which he himself was exposed by bearing letters; to renounce the plan if he wavered, and to accept it if its terrors did not deter him. I walked about till I heard the words of the song:—*Sognai mi gera un gato, E ti me carezzevi*. It was Tremerello bringing me my coffee. I acquainted him with my scruples and spared nothing to excite his fears. I found him staunch in his desire to *serve*, as he said, *two such complete gentlemen*. This was strangely at variance with the sheep's face he wore, and the name we had just given him.* Well, I was as firm on my part.

"I shall leave you my wine," said I, "see to find me the paper; I want to carry on this correspondence; and, rely on it, if any one comes without the warning song, I shall make an end of every suspicious article."

"Here is a sheet of paper ready for you; I will give you more whenever you please, and am perfectly satisfied of your prudence."

I longed to take my coffee; Tremerello left me, and I sat down to write. Did I do right? was the motive really approved by God? Was it not rather the triumph of my natural courage, of my preference of that which pleased me, instead of obeying the call for painful sacrifices. Mingled with this was a proud complacency, in return for the esteem expressed towards me by the unknown, and a fear of appearing cowardly, if I were to adhere to silence and decline a correspondence, every way so fraught with peril. How was I to resolve these doubts? I explained them frankly to my fellow-prisoner in replying to him, stating it nevertheless, as my opinion, that if anything were undertaken from good motives, and without the least repugnance of conscience, there could be no fear of blame. I advised him at the same time to reflect seriously upon the subject, and to express clearly with what degree of tranquillity, or of anxiety, he was prepared to engage in it. Moreover, if, upon reconsideration, he considered the plan as too dangerous, we ought to have firmness enough to renounce the satisfaction we promised ourselves in such a correspondence, and rest satisfied with the acquaintance we had formed, the mutual pleasure we had already derived, and the unalterable goodwill we felt towards each other, which resulted from it. I filled four pages with my explanations, and expressions of the warmest friendship; I briefly alluded to

* Tremerello, or the little trembler.

the subject of my imprisonment; I spoke of my family with enthusiastic love, as well as of some of my friends, and attempted to draw a full picture of my mind and character.

In the evening I sent the letter. I had not slept during the preceding night; I was completely exhausted, and I soon fell into a profound sleep, from which I awoke on the ensuing morning, refreshed and comparatively happy. I was in hourly expectation of receiving my new friend's answer, and I felt at once anxious and pleased at the idea.

CHAPTER XXXVI.

THE answer was brought with my coffee. I welcomed Tremerello, and, embracing him, exclaimed, "May God reward you for this goodness!" My suspicions had fled, because they were hateful to me; and because, making a point of never speaking imprudently upon politics, they appeared equally useless; and because, with all my admiration for the genius of Tacitus, I had never much faith in the justice of *tacitising* as he does, and of looking upon every object on the dark side. Giuliano (as the writer signed himself), began his letter with the usual compliments, and informed me that he felt not the least anxiety in entering upon the correspondence. He rallied me upon my hesitation; occasionally assumed a tone of irony; and then more seriously declared that it had given him no little pain to observe in me "a certain scrupulous wavering, and a subtilty of conscience, which, however Christian-like, was little in accordance with true philosophy." "I shall continue to esteem you," he added, "though we should not agree upon that point; for I am bound, in all sincerity, to inform you, that I have no religion, that I abhor all creeds, and that I assume from a feeling of modesty the name of Julian, from the circumstance of that good emperor having been so decided an enemy of the Christians, though, in fact,

I go much further than he ever did. The sceptred Julian believed in God, and had his own little superstitions. I have none; I believe not in a God, but refer all virtue to the love of truth, and the hatred of such as do not please me." There was no reasoning in what he said. He inveighed bitterly against Christianity, made an idol of worldly honour and virtue; and in a half serious and jocular vein took on himself to pronounce the Emperor Julian's eulogium for his apostasy, and his philanthropic efforts to eradicate all traces of the gospel from the face of the earth.

Apprehending that he had thus given too severe a shock to my opinions, he then asked my pardon, attempting to excuse himself upon the ground of *perfect sincerity.* Reiterating his extreme wish to enter into more friendly relations with me, he then bade me farewell.

In a postscript he added:—"I have no sort of scruples, except a fear of not having made myself sufficiently understood. I ought not to conceal that to me the Christian language which you employ, appears a mere mask to conceal your real opinions. I wish it may be so; and in this case, throw off your cloak, as I have set you an example."

I cannot describe the effect this letter had upon me. I had opened it full of hope and ardour. Suddenly an icy hand seemed to chill the life-blood of my heart. That sarcasm on my conscientiousness hurt me extremely. I repented having formed any acquaintance with such a man, I who so much detest the doctrine of the cynics, who consider it so wholly unphilosophical, and the most injurious in its tendency: I who despise all kind of arrogance as it deserves.

Having read the last word it contained, I took the letter in both my hands, and tearing it directly down the middle, I held up a half in each like an executioner, employed in exposing it to public scorn.

CHAPTER XXXVII.

I KEPT my eye fixed on the fragments, meditating for a moment upon the inconstancy and fallacy of human things. I had just before eagerly desired to obtain, that which I now tore with disdain. I had hoped to have found a companion in misfortune, and how I should have valued his friendship! Now I gave him all kinds of hard names, insolent, arrogant, atheist, and self-condemned.

I repeated the same operation, dividing the wretched members of the guilty letter again and again, till happening to cast my eye on a piece remaining in my hand, expressing some better sentiment, I changed my intention, and collecting together the *disjecta membra*, ingeniously pieced them with the view of reading it once more. I sat down, placed them on my great Bible, and examined the whole. I then got up, walked about, read, and thought, "If I do not answer," said I, "he will think he has terrified me at the mere appearance of such a philosophical hero, a very Hercules in his own estimation. Let us show him, with all due courtesy, that we fear not to confront him and his vicious doctrines, any more than to brave the risk of a correspondence, more dangerous to others than to ourselves. I will teach him that true courage does not consist in ridiculing *conscience*, and that real dignity does not consist in arrogance and pride. He shall be taught the reasonableness of Christianity, and the nothingness of disbelief. Moreover, if this mock Julian start opinions so directly opposite to my own, if he spare not the most biting sarcasm, if he attack me thus uncourteously; is it not all a proof that he can be no spy? Yet, might not this be a mere stratagem, to draw me into a discussion by wounding my self-love? Yet no! I am unjust—I smart under his bitter irreligious jests, and conclude at once that he must be the most infamous of men. Base suspicion, which I have so often decried in others! he may be what he appears—a presumptuous infidel, but not a spy. Have I even a right to call by the name of *insolence*, what he considers *sincerity*. Is this, I continued, thy humility, oh, hypocrite? If any one presume to maintain his own opinions, and to question your faith, he is forthwith to be met with contempt and abuse. Is not this worse in a Christian, than the bold sincerity of the unbeliever? Yes, and perhaps he only requires one ray of Divine grace, to employ his noble energetic love of truth in the cause of true religion, with far greater success than yourself. Were it not, then, more becoming in me to pray for, than to irritate him? Who knows, but while employed in destroying his letter with every mark of ignominy, he might be reading mine with expressions of kindness and affection; never dreaming I should fly into such a mighty passion at his plain and bold sincerity. Is he not the better of the two, to love and esteem me while declaring he is no Christian; than I who exclaim, I am a Christian, and I detest you. It is difficult to obtain a knowledge of a man during a long intercourse, yet I would condemn him on the evidence of a single letter. He may, perhaps, be unhappy in his atheism, and wish to hear all my arguments to enable him the better to arrive at the truth. Perhaps, too, I may be called to effect so beneficent a work, the humble instrument of a gracious God. Oh, that it may indeed be so, I will not shrink from the task."

CHAPTER XXXVIII.

I SAT down to write to Julian, and was cautious not to let one irritating word proceed from my pen. I took in good part his reflection upon my fastidiousness of conscience; I even joked about it, telling him he perhaps gave me too much credit for it, and ought to suspend his good opinion till he knew me better. I praised his sincerity, assuring him that he would find me equal to him in this respect, and that as a proof of it, I had determined to defend Christianity, "Well persuaded," I added, "that as I shall readily give free scope to your opinions, you will be prepared to give me the same advantage."

I then boldly entered upon my task, arguing my way by degrees, and analysing with impartiality the essence of Christianity; the worship of God free from superstitions, the brotherhood of mankind, aspiration after virtue, humility without baseness, dignity without pride, as exemplified in our Divine Saviour! what more philosophical, and more truly grand?

It was next my object to demonstrate, "that this divine wisdom had more or less displayed itself to all those who by the light of reason had sought after the truth, though not generally diffused till the arrival of its great Author upon the earth. He had proved his heavenly mission by effecting the most wonderful and glorious results, by human means the most mean and humble. What the greatest philosophers had in vain attempted, the overthrow of idolatry, and the universal preaching of love and brotherhood, was achieved by a few untutored missionaries. From that era was first dated the emancipation of slaves, no less from bondage of limbs than of mind, until by degrees a civilisation without slavery became apparent, a state of society believed to be utterly impracticable by the ancient philosophers. A review of history from the appearance of Christ to the present age, would finally demonstrate that the religion he established had invariably been found adapted to all possible grades in civilised society. For this reason, the assertion that the gospel was no longer in accordance with the continued progress of civilisation, could not for a moment be maintained."

I wrote in as small characters as I could, and at great length, but I could not embrace all which I had ready prepared upon the subject. I re-examined the whole carefully. There was not one revengeful, injurious, or even repulsive word. Benevolence, toleration, and forbearance, were the only weapons I employed against ridicule and sarcasm of every kind; they were also employed after mature deliberation, and dictated from the heart.

I despatched the letter, and in no little anxiety waited the arrival of the next morning, in hopes of a speedy reply.

Tremerello came, and observed; "The gentleman, sir, was not able to write, but entreats of you to continue the joke."

"The joke!" I exclaimed. "No, he could not have said that! you must have mistaken him."

Tremerello shrugged up his shoulders: "I suppose I must, if you say so."

"But did it really seem as if he had said a joke?"

"As plainly as I now hear the sound of St. Mark's clock;" (the *Campanone* was just then heard.) I drank my coffee and was silent.

"But tell me; did he read the whole of the letter?"

"I think he did; for he laughed like a madman, and then squeezing your letter into a ball, he began to throw it about, till reminding him that he must not forget to destroy it, he did so immediately."

"That is very well."

I then put my coffee cup into Tremerello's hands, observing that it was plain the coffee had been made by the Siora Bettina.

"What! is it so bad?"

"Quite vile!"

"Well! I made it myself; and I can assure you that I made it strong; there were no dregs."

"True; it may be, my mouth is out of taste."

CHAPTER XXXIX.

I WALKED about the whole morning in a rage. "What an abandoned wretch is this Julian! what, call my letter a joke! play at ball with it, reply not a single line! But all your infidels are alike! They dare not stand the test of argument; they know their weakness, and try to turn it off with a jest. Full of vanity and boasting, they venture not to examine even themselves. They philosophers, indeed! worthy disciples of Democritus; who *did* nothing but laugh, and *was* nothing but a buffoon. I am rightly served, however, for beginning a correspondence like this; and still more for writing a second time."

At dinner, Tremerello took up my wine, poured it into a flask, and put it into his pocket, observing: "I see that you are in want of paper;" and he gave me some. He retired, and the moment I cast my eye on the paper, I felt tempted to sit down and write to Julian a sharp lecture on his intolerable turpitude and presumption, and so take leave of him. But again, I repented of my own violence, and uncharitableness, and finally resolved to write another letter in a better spirit as I had done before.

I did so, and despatched it without delay. The next morning I received a few lines, simply expressive of the writer's thanks; but without a single jest, or the least invitation to continue the correspondence. Such a billet displeased me; nevertheless I determined to persevere. Six long letters were the result, for each of which I received a few laconic lines of thanks, with some declamation against his enemies, followed by a joke on the abuse he had heaped upon them, asserting that it was extremely natural the strong should oppress the weak, and regretting that he was not in the list of the former. He then related some of his love affairs, and observed that they exercised no little sway over his disturbed imagination.

In reply to my last on the subject of Christianity, he said he had prepared a long letter; for which I looked out in vain, though he wrote to me every day on other topics—chiefly a tissue of obscenity and folly.

I reminded him of his promise that he would answer all my arguments, and recommended him to weigh well the reasonings with which I had supplied him before he attempted to write. He replied to this somewhat in a rage, assuming the airs of a philosopher, a man of firmness, a man who stood in no want of brains to distinguish "a hawk from a hand-saw."* He then resumed his jocular vein, and began to enlarge upon his experiences in life, and especially some very scandalous love adventures.

CHAPTER XL.

I BORE all this patiently, to give him no handle for accusing me of bigotry or intolerance, and in the hope that after the fever of erotic buffoonery and folly had subsided, he might have some lucid intervals, and listen to common sense. Meantime I gave him expressly to understand that I disapproved of his want of respect towards women, his free and profane expressions, and pitied those unhappy ones, who, he informed me, had been his victims.

He pretended to care little about my disapprobation, and repeated: "spite of your fine strictures upon immorality, I know well you are amused with the account of my adventures. All men are as fond of pleasure as I am, but they have not the frankness to talk of it without cloaking it from the eyes of the world; I will go on till you are quite enchanted, and confess yourself compelled in *very conscience* to applaud me." So he went on from week to week, I bearing with him, partly out of curiosity and partly in the

* Per capire che le lucciole non erano lanterne.

"To know that glowworms are not lanterns."

expectation he would fall upon some better topic; and I can fairly say that this species of tolerance, did me no little harm. I began to lose my respect for pure and noble truths, my thoughts became confused, and my mind disturbed. To converse with men of degraded minds is in itself degrading, at least if you possess not virtue very superior to mine. "This is a proper punishment," said I, "for my presumption; this it is to assume the office of a missionary without its sacredness of character."

One day I determined to write to him as follows:—"I have hitherto attempted to turn your attention to other subjects, and you persevere in sending me accounts of yourself which no way please me. For the sake of variety, let us correspond a little respecting worthier matters; if not, give the hand of fellowship, and let us have done."

The two ensuing days I received no answer, and I was glad of it. "Oh, blessed solitude;" often I exclaimed, "how far holier and better art thou than harsh and undignified association with the living. Away with the empty and impious vanities, the base actions, the low despicable conversations of such a world. I have studied it enough; let me turn to my communion with God; to the calm, dear recollections of my family and my true friends. I will read my Bible oftener than I have done, I will again write down my thoughts, will try to raise and improve them, and taste the pleasure of a sorrow at least innocent: a thousand fold to be preferred to vulgar and wicked imaginations."

Whenever Tremerello now entered my room he was in the habit of saying, "I have got no answer yet."

"It is all right," was my reply.

About the third day from this, he said, with a serious look, "Signor N. N. is rather indisposed."

"What is the matter with him?"

"He does not say, but he has taken to his bed, neither eats nor drinks, and is sadly out of humour."

I was touched; he was suffering and had no one to console him.

"I will write him a few lines," exclaimed I.

"I will take them this evening, then," said Tremerello, and he went out.

I was a little perplexed on sitting down to my table: "Am I right in resuming this correspondence? was I not, just now, praising solitude as a treasure newly found? what inconsistency is this! Ah! but he neither eats nor drinks, and I fear must be very ill. Is it, then, a moment to abandon him? My last letter was severe, and may perhaps have caused him pain. Perhaps, in spite of our different ways of thinking, he wished not to end our correspondence. Yes, he has thought my letter more caustic than I meant it to be, and taken it in the light of an absolute and contemptuous dismission.

CHAPTER XLI.

I SAT down and wrote as follows:—

"I hear that you are not well, and am extremely sorry for it. I wish I were with you, and enabled to assist you as a friend. I hope your illness is the sole cause why you have not written to me during the last three days. Did you take offence at my little strictures the other day? Believe me they were dictated by no ill will or spleen, but with the single object of drawing your attention to more serious subjects. Should it be irksome for you to write, send me an exact account, by word, how you find yourself. You shall hear from me every day, and I will try to say something to amuse you, and to show you that I really wish you well."

Imagine my unfeigned surprise when I received an answer, couched in these terms:

"I renounce your friendship: if you are at a loss how to estimate mine, I return the compliment in its full force. I am not a man to put up with injurious treatment; I am not one, who, once rejected, will be ordered to return.

"Because you heard I was unwell, you approach me with a hypocritical air, in the idea that illness will break down my spirit, and make me listen to your sermons . . ."

In this way he rambled on, reproaching and despising me in the most revolting terms he could find, and turning every thing I had said into ridicule and burlesque. He assured me that he knew how to live and die with consistency; that is to say, with the utmost hatred and contempt for all philosophical creeds differing from his own. I was dismayed!

"A pretty conversion I have made of it!" I exclaimed; "yet God is my witness that my motives were pure. I have done nothing to merit an attack like this. But patience! I am once more undeceived. I am not called upon to do more."

In a few days I became less angry, and conceived that all this bitterness might have resulted from some excitement which might pass away. Probably he repents, yet scorns to confess he was in the wrong. In such a state of mind, it might be generous of me to write to him once more. It cost my self-love something, but I did it. To humble one's self for a good purpose is not degrading, with whatever degree of unjust contempt it may be returned.

I received a reply less violent, but not less insulting. The implacable patient declared that he admired what he called my evangelical moderation. "Now, therefore," he continued, "let us resume our correspondence, but let us speak out. We do not like each other, but we will write, each for his own amusement, setting everything down which may come into our heads. You will tell me your seraphic visions and revelations, and I will treat you with my profane adventures; you again will run into ecstasies upon the dignity of man, yea, and of woman; I into an ingenuous narrative of my various profanations; I hoping to make a convert of you, and you of me.

"Give me an answer should you approve these conditions."

"I replied, "Yours is not a compact, but a jest. I was full of good-will towards you. My conscience does not constrain me to do more than to wish you every happiness both as regards this and another life."

Thus ended my secret connexion with that strange man. But who knows; he was perhaps more exasperated by ill fortune, delirium, or despair, than really bad at heart.

CHAPTER XLII.

I ONCE more learnt to value solitude, and my days tracked each other without any distinction or mark of change.

The summer was over; it was towards the close of September, and the heat grew less oppressive; October came. I congratulated myself now on occupying a chamber well adapted for winter. One morning, however, the jailer made his appearance, with an order to change my prison.

"And where am I to go?"

"Only a few steps, into a fresher chamber."

"But why not think of it when I was dying of suffocation; when the air was filled with gnats, and my bed with bugs?"

"The order did not come before."

"Patience! let us be gone!"

Notwithstanding I had suffered so greatly in this prison, it gave me pain to leave it; not simply because it would have been best for the winter season, but for many other reasons. There I had the ants to attract my attention, which I had fed and looked upon, I may almost say, with paternal care. Within the last few days, however, my friend the spider, and my great ally in my war with the gnats, had, for some reason or other, chosen to emigrate; at least he did not come as usual. "Yet perhaps," said I, "he may remember me, and come back, but he will find my prison empty, or occupied by some other guest—no friend perhaps to spiders—and thus meet with an awkward reception. His fine woven house, and his gnat-feasts will all be put an end to."

Again, my gloomy abode had been embellished by the presence of Angiola, so good, so gentle and compassionate. There she used to sit, and try every means she could devise to amuse me, even dropping crumbs of bread for my little visitors, the ants; and there I heard her sobs, and saw the tears fall thick and fast, as she spoke of her cruel lover.

The place I was removed to was under the leaden prisons, (*I Piombi*) open to the north and west, with two windows, one on each side; an abode exposed to perpetual cold and even icy chill during the severest months. The window to the west was the largest, that to the north was high and narrow, and situated above my bed.

I first looked out at this last, and found that it commanded a view of the Palace of the Patriarch. Other prisons were near mine, in a narrow wing to the right, and in a projection of the building right opposite. Here were two prisons, one above the other. The lower had an enormous window, through which I could see a man, very richly drest, pacing to and fro. It was the Signor Caporale di Cesena. He perceived me, made a signal, and we pronounced each other's names.

I next looked out at my other window. I put the little table upon my bed, and a chair upon my table; I climbed up and found myself on a level with part of the palace roof; and beyond this was to be seen a fine view of the city and the lake.

I paused to admire it; and though I heard some one open the door, I did not move. It was the jailer; and perceiving that I had clambered up, he got it into his head I was making an attempt to escape, forgetting, in his alarm, that I was not a mouse to creep through all those narrow bars. In a moment he sprung upon the bed, spite of a violent sciatica which had nearly bent him double, and catching me by the legs, he began to call out, "thieves and murder!"

"But don't you see," I exclaimed, "you thoughtless man, that I cannot conjure myself through these horrible bars? Surely you know I got up here out of mere curiosity."

"Oh, yes, I see, I apprehend, sir; but quick, sir, jump down, sir; these are all temptations of the devil to make you think of it! come down, sir, pray."

I lost no time in my descent, and laughed.

CHAPTER XLIII.

At the windows of the side prisons I recognised six other prisoners, all there on account of politics. Just then, as I was composing my mind to perfect solitude, I found myself comparatively in a little world of human beings around me. The change was, at first, irksome to me, such complete seclusion having rendered me almost unsociable, add to which, the disagreeable termination of my correspondence with Julian. Still, the little conversation I was enabled to carry on, partly by signs, with my new fellow-prisoners, was of advantage by diverting my attention. I breathed not a word respecting my correspondence with Julian; it was a point of honour between us, and in bringing it forward here, I was fully aware that in the immense number of unhappy men with which these prisons were thronged, it would be impossible to ascertain who was the assumed Julian.

To the interest derived from seeing my fellow-captives

was added another of a yet more delightful kind. I could perceive from my large window, beyond the projection of prisons, situated right before me, a surface of roofs, decorated with cupolas, *campanili*, towers, and chimneys, which gradually faded in a distant view of sea and sky. In the house nearest to me, a wing of the Patriarchal palace, lived an excellent family, who had a claim to my gratitude, for expressing, by their salutations, the interest which they took in my fate. A sign, a word of kindness to the unhappy, is really charity of no trivial kind. From one of the windows I saw a little boy, nine or ten years old, stretching out his hands towards me, and I heard him call out, "Mamma, mamma, they have placed somebody up there in the Piombi. Oh, you poor prisoner, who are you?"

"I am Silvio Pellico," was the reply.

Another older boy now ran to the same window, and cried out, "Are you Silvio Pellico?"

"Yes; and tell me your names, dear boys."

"My name is Antonio S——, and my brother's is Joseph."

He then turned round, and, speaking to some one within, "What else ought I to ask him?" A lady, whom I conjecture to have been their mother, then half concealed, suggested some pretty words to them, which they repeated, and for which I thanked them with all my heart. These sort of communications were a small matter, yet it required to be cautious how we indulged in them, lest we should attract the notice of the jailer. Morning, noon, and night, they were a source of the greatest consolation; the little boys were constantly in the habit of bidding me good night, before the windows were closed, and the lights brought in, "Good night, Silvio," and often it was repeated by the good lady, in a more subdued voice, "Good night, Silvio, have courage!"

When engaged at their meals they would say, "How we

wish we could give you any of this good coffee and milk. Pray remember, the first day they let you out, to come and see us. Mamma and we will give you plenty of good things,* and as many kisses as you like."

CHAPTER XLIV.

THE month of October brought round one of the most disagreeable anniversaries in my life. I was arrested on the 13th of that month in the preceding year. Other recollections of the same period, also pained me. That day two years, a highly valued and excellent man whom I truly honoured, was drowned in the Ticino. Three years before, a young person, Odoardo Briche,† whom I loved as if he had been my own son, had accidentally killed himself with a musket. Earlier in my youth another severe affliction had befallen me in the same month.

Though not superstitious, the remembrance of so many unhappy occurrences at the same period of the year, inspired a feeling of extreme sorrow. While conversing at the window with the children, and with my fellow prisoners, I assumed an air of mirth, but hardly had I re-entered my cave than an irresistible feeling of melancholy weighed down every faculty of my mind. In vain I attempted to engage in some literary composition; I was involuntarily impelled to write upon other topics. I thought of my family, and wrote letters after letters, in which I poured forth all my burdened spirit, all I had felt and enjoyed of home, in far happier days, surrounded by brothers, sisters, and friends who had always loved me. The desire of seeing them, and

* Buzzolai, a kind of small loaf.

† Odoardo Briche, a young man of truly animated genius, and the most amiable disposition. He was the son of Mous. Briche, member of the Constituent Assemby in France, who for thirty years past, had selected Milan as his adopted country.

long compulsory separation, led me to speak on a variety of little things, and reveal a thousand thoughts of gratitude and tenderness, which would not otherwise have occurred to my mind.

In the same way I took a review of my former life, diverting my attention by recalling past incidents, and dwelling upon those happier periods now for ever fled. Often, when the picture I had thus drawn, and sat contemplating for hours, suddenly vanished from my sight, and left me conscious only of the fearful present, and more threatening future, the pen fell from my hand; I recoiled with horror; the contrast was more than I could bear. These were terrific moments; I had already felt them, but never with such intense susceptibility as then. It was agony. This I attributed to extreme excitement of the passions, occasioned by expressing them in the form of letters, addressed to persons to whom I was so tenderly attached.

I turned to other subjects, I determined to change the form of expressing my ideas, but could not. In whatever way I began, it always ended in a letter teeming with affection and with grief.

"What," I exclaimed, "am *I* no more master of my own will? Is this strange necessity of doing that which I object to, a distortion of my brain? At first I could have accounted for it; but after being inured to this solitude, reconciled, and supported by religious reflections; how have I become the slave of these blind impulses, these wanderings of heart and mind? let me apply to other matters!" I then endeavoured to pray; or to weary my attention by hard study of the German. Alas! I commenced and found myself actually engaged in writing a letter!

CHAPTER XLV.

SUCH a state of mind was a real disease, or I know not if it may be called a kind of somnambulism. Without doubt it was the effect of extreme lassitude, occasioned by continual thought and watchfulness.

It gained upon me. I grew feverish and sleepless. I left off coffee, but the disease was not removed. It appeared to me as if I were two persons, one of them eagerly bent upon writing letters, the other upon doing something else. "At least," said I, "you shall write them in German if you do; and we shall learn a little of the language. Methought *he* then set to work, and wrote volumes of bad German, and he certainly brought me rapidly forward in the study of it. Towards morning, my mind being wholly exhausted, I fell into a heavy stupor, during which all those most dear to me haunted my dreams. I thought that my father and mother were weeping over me; I heard their lamentations, and suddenly I started out of my sleep sobbing and affrighted. Sometimes, during short, disturbed slumbers, I heard my mother's voice, as if consoling others, with whom she came into my prison, and she addressed me in the most affectionate language upon the duty of resignation, and then, when I was rejoiced to see her courage, and that of others, suddenly she appeared to burst into tears, and all wept. I can convey no idea of the species of agony which I at these times felt.

To escape from this misery, I no longer went to bed. I sat down to read by the light of my lamp, but I could comprehend nothing, and soon I found that I was even unable to think. I next tried to copy something, but still copied something different from what I was writing, always recurring to the subject of my afflictions. If I retired to rest, it was worse; I could lie in no position; I became convulsed, and was constrained to rise. In case I slept, the same visions reappeared, and made me suffer much more than I did by keeping awake. My prayers, too, were feeble and ineffectual; and, at length, I could simply invoke the name of the Deity; of the Being who had assumed a human form, and was acquainted with grief. I was afraid to sleep; my prayers seemed to bring me no relief; my imagination became excited, and, even when awake, I heard strange noises close to me, sometimes sighs and groans, at others mingled with sounds of stifled laughter. I was never superstitious, but these apparently real and unaccountable sights and sounds led me to doubt, and I then firmly believed that I was the victim of some unknown and malignant beings. Frequently I took my light, and made a search for those mockers and persecutors of my waking and sleeping hours. At last they began to pull me by my clothes, threw my books upon the ground, blew out my lamp, and even, as it seemed, conveyed me into another dungeon. I would then start to my feet, look and examine all round me, and ask myself if I were really mad. The actual world, and that of my imagination, were no longer distinguishable, I knew not whether what I saw and felt was a delusion or truth. In this horrible state I could only repeat one prayer, "My God, my God, why hast thou forsaken me?"

CHAPTER XLVI.

One morning early, I threw myself upon my pallet, having first placed my handkerchief, as usual, under my pillow. Shortly after, falling asleep, I suddenly woke, and found myself in a state of suffocation; my persecutors were strangling me, and, on putting my hand to my throat, I actually found my own handkerchief, all knotted, tied round my neck. I could have sworn I had never made those knots; yet I must have done this in my delirium; but as it was then impossible to believe it, I lived in continual expectation of being strangled. The recollection is still horrible. They left me at dawn of day; and, resuming my courage, I no longer felt the least apprehension, and even imagined it would be impossible they should again return. Yet no sooner did the night set in, than I was again haunted by them in all their horrors; being made sensible of their gradual approach by cold shiverings, the loss of all power, with a species of fascination which riveted both the eye and the mind. In fact, the more weak and wretched I felt, at night, the greater were my efforts during the day to appear cheerful in conversing with my companions, with the two boys at the palace, and with my jailers. No one to hear my jokes, would have imagined it possible that I was suffering under the disease I did. I thought to encourage myself by this forced merriment, but the spectral visions which I laughed at by day became fearful realities in the hours of darkness.

Had I dared, I should have petitioned the commission to change my apartment, but the fear of ridicule, in case I should be asked my reasons, restrained me. No reasonings, no studies, or pursuits, and even no prayers, were longer of avail, and the idea of being wholly abandoned by heaven, took possession of my mind.

All those wicked sophisms against a just Providence, which, while in possession of reason, had appeared to me so vain and impious, now recurred with redoubled power, in the form of irresistible arguments. I struggled mightily against this last and greatest evil I had yet borne, and in the lapse of a few days the temptation fled. Still I refused to acknowledge the truth and beauty of religion; I quoted the assertions of the most violent atheists, and those which Julian had so recently dwelt upon: "Religion serves only to enfeeble the mind," was one of these, and I actually presumed that by renouncing my God I should acquire greater fortitude. Insane idea! I denied God, yet knew not how to deny those invisible malevolent beings, that appeared to encompass me, and feast upon my sufferings.

What shall I call this martyrdom? is it enough to say that it was a disease? or was it a divine chastisement for my pride, to teach me that without a special illumination I might become as great an unbeliever as Julian, and still more absurd. However this may be, it pleased God to deliver me from such evil, when I least expected it. One morning, after taking my coffee, I was seized with violent sickness, attended with colic. I imagined that I had been poisoned. After excessive vomiting, I burst into a strong perspiration and retired to bed. About mid-day I fell asleep, and continued in a quiet slumber till evening. I awoke in great surprise at this unexpected repose, and, thinking I should not sleep again, I got up. On rising I said, "I shall now have more fortitude to resist my accustomed terrors." But they returned no more. I was in ecstasies; I threw myself upon my knees in the fulness of my heart, and again prayed to my God in spirit and in truth, beseeching pardon for having denied, during many days, His holy name. It was almost too much for my newly reviving strength, and while even yet upon my knees, supporting my head against a chair, I fell into a profound sleep in that very position.

Some hours afterwards, as I conjectured, I seemed in part to awake, but no sooner had I stretched my weary limbs upon my rude couch than I slept till the dawn of day. The same disposition to somnolency continued through the day, and the next night, I rested as soundly as before. What was the sort of crisis that had thus taken place? I know not; but I was perfectly restored.

CHAPTER XLVII.

The sickness of the stomach which I had so long laboured under now ceased, the pains of the head also left me, and I felt an extraordinary appetite. My digestion was good, and I gained strength. Wonderful providence! that deprived me of my health to humble my mind, and again restored it when the moment was at hand that I should require it all, that I might not sink under the weight of my sentence.

On the 24th of November, one of our companions, Dr. Foresti, was taken from the *Piombi*, and transported no one knew whither. The jailer, his wife, and the assistants, were alike alarmed, and not one of them ventured to throw the least light upon this mysterious affair.

"And why should you persist," said Tremerello, "in wishing to know, when nothing good is to be heard? I have told you too much—too much already."

"Then what is the use of trying to hide it? I know it too well. He is condemned to death."

"Who?....he....Doctor Foresti?"

Tremerello hesitated, but the love of gossip was not the least of his virtues.

"Don't say, then," he resumed, "that I am a babbler; I never wished to say a word about these matters; so, remember, it is you who compel me."

"Yes, yes, I do compel you; but courage! tell me every thing you know respecting the poor Doctor?"

"Ah, Sir! they have made him cross the Bridge of Sighs! he lies in the dungeons of the condemned; sentence of death has been announced to him and two others."

"And will it be executed? When? Oh, unhappy man! and what are the others' names?"

"I know no more. The sentences have not been published. It is reported in Venice that they will be commuted. I trust in God they may, at least, as regards the good Doctor. Do you know, I am as fond of that noble fellow, pardon the expression, as if he were my own brother."

He seemed moved, and walked away. Imagine the agitation I suffered throughout the whole of that day, and indeed long after, as there were no means of ascertaining anything further respecting the fate of these unfortunate men.

A month elapsed, and at length the sentences connected with the first trial were published. Nine were condemned to death, *graciously* exchanged for hard imprisonment, some for twenty, and others for fifteen years in the fortress of Spielberg, near the city of Brunn, in Moravia; while those for ten years and under were to be sent to the fortress of Lubiana.

Were we authorised to conclude, from this commutation of sentence in regard to those first condemned, that the parties subject to the second trial would likewise be spared? Was the indulgence to be confined only to the former, on account of their having been arrested previous to the publication of the edicts against secret societies; the full vengeance of the law being reserved for subsequent offenders?

Well, I exclaimed, we shall not long be kept in suspense; I am at least grateful to Heaven for being allowed time to prepare myself in a becoming manner for the final scene.

CHAPTER XLVIII.

It was now my only consideration how to die like a Christian, and with proper fortitude. I felt, indeed, a strong temptation to avoid the scaffold by committing suicide, but overcame it. What merit is there in refusing to die by the hand of the executioner, and yet to fall by one's own? To save one's honour? But is it not childish to suppose that there can be more honour in cheating the executioner, than in not doing this, when it is clear that we must die. Even had I not been a Christian, upon serious reflection, suicide would have appeared to me both ridiculous and useless, if not criminal in a high degree.

"If the term of life be expired," continued I, "am I not fortunate in being permitted to collect my thoughts and purify my conscience with penitence and prayer becoming a man in affliction. In popular estimation, the being led to the scaffold is the worst part of death; in the opinion of the wise, is not this far preferable to the thousand deaths which daily occur by disease, attended by general prostration of intellect, without power to raise the thoughts from the lowest state of physical exhaustion."

I felt the justice of this reasoning, and lost all feeling of anxiety or terror at the idea of a public execution. I reflected deeply on the sacraments calculated to support me under such an appalling trial, and I felt disposed to receive them in a right spirit. Should I have been enabled, had I really been conducted to the scaffold, to preserve the same elevation of mind, the same forgiveness of my enemies, the same readiness to lay down my life at the will of God, as I then felt? Alas, how inconsistent is man! when most firm and pious, how liable is he to fall suddenly into weakness and crime! Is it likely I should have died worthily? God only knows; I dare not think well enough of myself to assert it.

The probable approach of death so riveted my imagination, that not only did it seem possible but as if marked by an infallible presentiment. I no longer indulged a hope of avoiding it, and at every sound of footsteps and keys, or the opening of my door, I was in the habit of exclaiming: "Courage! Perhaps I am going to receive sentence. Let me hear it with calm dignity, and bless the name of the Lord."

I considered in what terms I should last address my

family, each of my brothers, and each of my sisters, and by revolving in my mind these sacred and affecting duties, I was often drowned in tears, without losing my fortitude and resignation.

I was naturally unable to enjoy sound repose; but my sleeplessness was not of the same alarming character as before; no visions, spectres, or concealed enemies were ready to deprive me of life. I spent the night in calm and reviving prayer. Towards morning I was enabled to sleep for about two hours, and rose late to breakfast.

One night I had retired to rest earlier than usual; I had hardly slept a quarter of an hour, when I awoke, and beheld an immense light upon the wall opposite to me. At first I imagined that I had been seized with my former illness; but this was no illusion. The light shone through the north window, under which I then lay.

I started up, seized my table, placed it on my bed, and a chair again upon the table, by means of all which I mounted up, and beheld one of the most terrific spectacles of fire that can be imagined. It was not more than a musket shot distant from our prison; it proceeded from the establishment of the public ovens, and the edifice was entirely consumed.

The night was exceedingly dark, and vast globes of flame spouted forth on both sides, borne away by a violent wind. All around, it seemed as if the sky rained sparks of fire. The adjacent lake reflected the magnificent sight; numbers of gondolas went and came, but my sympathy was most excited at the danger and terrors of those who resided nearest to the burning edifice. I heard the far off voices of men and women calling to each other. Among others, I caught the name of Angiola, and of this doubtless there are some thousands in Venice: yet I could not help fearing it might be the one of whom the recollection was so sweet to me. Could it be her?—was she surrounded by the flames? how I longed to fly to her rescue.

Full of excitement, wonder, and terror, I stood at the window till the day dawned, I then got down oppressed by a feeling of deep sorrow, and imagined much greater misfortune than had really occurred. I was informed by Tremerello that only the ovens and the adjoining magazine had suffered, the loss consisting chiefly of corn and sacks of flour.

CHAPTER XLIX.

The effect of this accident upon my imagination had not yet ceased, when one night, as I was sitting at my little table reading, and half perished with cold, I heard a number of voices not far from me. They were those of the jailer, his wife, and sons, with the assistants, all crying: "Fire! fire. Oh, blessed Virgin! we are lost, we are lost!"

I felt no longer cold, I started to my feet in a violent perspiration, and looked out to discover the quarter from which the fire proceeded. I could perceive nothing, I was informed, however, that it arose in the palace itself, from some public chambers contiguous to the prisons. One of the assistants called out, "But, sir governor, what shall we do with these caged birds here, if the fire keeps a head?" The head jailer replied, "Why, I should not like to have them roasted alive. Yet I cannot let them out of their bars without special orders from the commission. You may run as fast as you can, and get an order if you can."

"To be sure I will, but, you know, it will be too late for the prisoners."

All this was said in the rude Venetian dialect, but I understood it too well. And now, where was all my heroic spirit and resignation, which I had counted upon to meet sudden death? Why did the idea of being burnt alive throw me into such a fever? I felt ashamed of this unworthy fear, and though just on the point of crying out to the jailer to let me out, I restrained myself, reflecting that there might be as little pleasure in being strangled as in being burnt. Still I felt really afraid.

"Here," said I, "is a specimen of my courage, should I escape the flames, and be doomed to mount the scaffold. I will restrain my fear, and hide it from others as well as I can, though I know I shall tremble. Yet surely it is courage to behave as if we were not afraid, whatever we may feel. Is it not generosity to give away that which it costs us much to part with? It is, also, an act of obedience, though we obey with great repugnance."

The tumult in the jailer's house was so loud and continued that I concluded the fire was on the increase. The messenger sent to ask permission for our temporary release had not returned. At last I thought I heard his voice; no; I listened, he is not come. Probably the permission will not be granted; there will be no means of escape; if the jailer should not humanely take the responsibility upon himself, we shall be suffocated in our dungeons! Well, but this, I exclaimed, is not philosophy, and it is not religion. Were it not better to prepare myself to witness the flames bursting into my chamber, and about to swallow me up.

Meantime the clamour seemed to diminish; by degrees it died away; was this any proof that the fire had ceased? Or, perhaps, all who could had already fled, and left the prisoners to their fate.

The silence continued, no flames appeared, and I retired to bed, reproaching myself for the want of fortitude I had evinced. Indeed, I began to regret that I had not been burnt alive, instead of being handed over, as a victim, into the hands of men.

The next morning, I learnt the real cause of the fire from Tremerello, and laughed at his account of the fear he had endured, as if my own had not been as great—perhaps, in fact, much greater of the two.

CHAPTER L.

On the 11th of January, 1822, about nine in the morning, Tremerello came into my room in no little agitation, and said,

"Do you know, Sir, that in the island of San Michele, a little way from Venice, there is a prison containing more than a hundred Carbonari."

"You have told me so a hundred times. Well! what would you have me hear, speak out; are some of them condemned?"

"Exactly."

"Who are they?"

"I don't know."

"Is my poor friend Maroncelli among them?"

"Ah, Sir, too many . . . I know not who." And he went away in great emotion, casting on me a look of compassion.

Shortly after came the jailer, attended by the assistants, and by a man whom I had never before seen. The latter opened his subject as follows: "The commission, Sir, has given orders that you come with me!"

"Let us go, then," I replied; "may I ask who you are?"

"I am jailer of the San Michele prisons, where I am going to take you."

The jailer of the *Piombi* delivered to the new governor the money belonging to me which he had in his hands. I obtained permission to make some little present to the under jailers; I then put my clothes in order, put my Bible under my arm, and departed. In descending the immense track of staircases, Tremerello for a moment took my hand; he pressed it as much as to say, "Unhappy man! you are lost."

We came out at a gate which opened upon the lake, and

there stood a gondola with two under jailers belonging to San Michele.

I entered the boat with feelings of the most contradictory nature; regret at leaving the prison of the *Piombi*, where I had suffered so much, but where I had become attached to some individuals, and they to me; the pleasure of beholding once more the sky, the city, and the clear waters, without the intervention of iron bars. Add to this the recollection of that joyous gondola, which, in time past, had borne me on the bosom of that placid lake; the gondolas of the lake of Como, those of Lago Maggiore, the little barks of the Po, those of the Rodano, and of the Sonna! Oh, happy vanished years! who, who then so happy in the world as I?

The son of excellent and affectionate parents, in a rank of life, perhaps, the happiest for the cultivation of the affections, being equally removed from riches and from poverty: I had spent my infancy in the participation of the sweetest domestic ties; had been the object of the tenderest domestic cares. I had subsequently gone to Lyons, to my maternal uncle, an elderly man, extremely wealthy, and deserving of all he possessed: and at his mansion I partook of all the advantages and delights of elegance and refined society, which gave an indescribable charm to those youthful days. Thence returning into Italy, under the parental roof, I at once devoted myself with ardour to study, and the enjoyment of society; everywhere meeting with distinguished friends and the most encouraging praise. Monti and Foscolo, although at variance with each other, were kind to me. I became more attached to the latter, and this irritable man, who, by his asperities, provoked so many to quarrel with him, was with me full of gentleness and cordiality. Other distinguished characters likewise became attached to me, and I returned all their regard. Neither envy nor calumny had the least influence over me, or I felt it only from persons who had not the power to injure me. On the fall of the kingdom of Italy, my father removed to Turin, with the rest of his family. I had preferred to remain at Milan, where I spent my time at once so profitably and so happily as made me unwilling to leave it. Here I had three friends to whom I was greatly attached—D. Pietro Borsieri, Lodovico di Breme, and the Count Luigi Porro Lambertenghi. Subsequently I added to them Count Federigo Confalonieri.* Becoming the preceptor of two young sons of Count Porro, I was to them as a father, and their father acted like a brother to me. His mansion was the resort not only of society the most refined and cultivated of Italy, but of numbers of celebrated strangers. It was there I became acquainted with De Stael, Schlegel, Davis, Byron, Brougham, Hobhouse, and illustrious travellers from all parts of Europe. How delightful, how noble an incentive to all that is great and good, is an intercourse with men of first-rate merit! I was then happy; I would not have exchanged my lot with a prince; and now, to be hurled, as I had been, from the summit of all my hopes and prospects, into an abyss of wretchedness, and to be hurried thus from dungeon to dungeon, to perish doubtless either by a violent death or lingering in chains.

* Respecting Pietro Borsieri, Lodovico di Breme, and Count Porro, mention has already been made. The Count Federico Confalonieri, of an illustrious family of Milan, a man of immense intellect, and the firmest courage, was also the most zealous promoter of popular institutions in Lombardy. The Austrian Government, becoming aware of the aversion entertained by the Count for the foreign yoke which pressed so heavily upon his country, had him seized and handed over to the special commissions, which sat in the years 1822 and 1823. By these he was condemned to the severest of all punishments—imprisonment for life, in the fortress of Spielberg, where, during six months of each weary year, he is compelled by the excess of his sufferings to lie stretched upon a wretched pallet, more dead than alive.

CHAPTER LI.

ABSORBED in reflections like these, I reached San Michele, and was locked up in a room which embraced a view of the court yard, of the lake, and the beautiful island of Murano. I inquired respecting Maroncelli from the jailer, from his wife, and the four assistants; but their visits were exceedingly brief, very ceremonious, and, in fact, they would tell me nothing.

Nevertheless where there are five or six persons, it is rarely you do not find one who possesses a compassionate, as well as a communicative disposition. I met with such a one, and from him I learnt what follows:—

Maroncelli, after having been long kept apart, had been placed with Count Camillo Laderchi.* The last, within a few days, had been declared innocent, and discharged from prison, and the former again remained alone. Some other of our companions had also been set at liberty; the Professor Romagnosi,† and Count Giovanni Arrivabene.‡ Captain

* The Count Camillo Laderchi, a member of one of the most distinguished families of Faenza, and formerly prefect in the ex-kingdom of Italy.

† Gian Domenico Romagnosi, a native of Piacenza, was for some years Professor of Criminal Law, in the University of Pavia. He is the author of several philosophical works, but more especially of the *Genesi del Diritto Penale*, which spread his reputation both throughout and beyond Italy. Though at an advanced age, he was repeatedly imprisoned and examined on the charge of having belonged to a lodge of Freemasons; a charge advanced against him by an ungrateful Tyrolese, who had initiated him into, and favoured him as a fellow-member of, the same society, and who had the audacity actually to sit as judge upon his *friend's* trial.

‡ The Count Giovanni Arrivabene, of Mantua, who, being in possession of considerable fortune, made an excellent use of it, both as regarded private acts of benevolence, and the maintenance of a school of mutual instruction. But having more recently fallen under the displeasure of the Government, he abandoned Italy, and during his exile employed himself in writing, with rare im-

Rezia * and the Signor Canova were together. Professor Ressi † was dying at that time, in a prison next to that of the two before mentioned. "It follows then," said I, "that the sentences of those not set at liberty must have arrived. How are they to be made known? Perhaps, poor Ressi will die; and will not be in a state to hear his sentence; is it true?"

"I believe it is."

Every day I inquired respecting the unhappy man. "He has lost his voice; he is rather better; he is delirious; he is nearly gone; he spits blood; he is dying;" were the usual replies; till at length came the last of all, "He is dead."

I shed a tear to his memory, and consoled myself with thinking that he died ignorant of the sentence which awaited him.

The day following, the 21st of February, 1822, the jailer came for me about ten o'clock, and conducted me into the Hall of the Commission. The members were all seated, but they rose; the President, the Inquisitor, and two assisting Judges.—The first, with a look of deep commiseration, acquainted me that my sentence had arrived; that it was a

partiality, and admirable judgment, a work which must be considered interesting to all engaged in alleviating the ills of humanity, both here and in other countries. It is entitled, *Delle Societa di Publica Beneficenza in Londra.*

* The Capitano Rezia, one of the best artillery officers in the Italian army, son of Professor Rezia, the celebrated anatomist, whose highly valuable preparations and specimens are to be seen in the Anatomical Museum at Pavia.

† The Professor Ressi, who occupied, during several years, the chair of Political Economy in the University at Pavia. He is the author of a respectable work, published under the title of *Economica della Specie Umana.* Having unfortunately attracted the suspicions of the Austrian police, he was seized and committed to a dungeon, in which he died, about a year from the period of his arrest, and while the special examinations of the alleged conspirators were being held.

terriblo one; but that the clemency of the Emperor had mitigated it.

The Inquisitor, fixing his eye on me, then read it:—'Silvio Pellico, condemned to death; the imperial decree is, that the sentence be commuted for fifteen years hard imprisonment in the fortress of Spielberg."

"The will of God be done!" was my reply.

It was really my intention to bear this horrible blow like a Christian, and neither to exhibit nor to feel resentment against any one whatever. The President then commended my state of mind, warmly recommending me to persevere in it, and that possibly by affording an edifying example, I might in a year or two be deemed worthy of receiving further favours from the imperial clemency.

Instead, however, of one or two, it was many years before the full sentence was remitted.

The other judges also spoke encouragingly to me. One of them, indeed, had appeared my enemy on my trial, accosting me in a courteous but ironical tone, while his look of insulting triumph seemed to belie his words. I would not make oath it was so, but my blood was then boiling, and I was trying to smother my passion. While they were praising me for my Christian patience, I had not a jot of it left me. "To-morrow," continued the Inquisitor, "I am sorry to say, you must appear and receive your sentence in public. It is a formality which cannot be dispensed with."

"Be it so!" I replied.

"From this time we grant you the company of your friend," he added. Then calling the jailer, he consigned me into his hands, ordering that I should be placed in the same dungeon with Maroncelli,

CHAPTER LII.

It was a delightful moment, when, after a separation of three months, and having suffered so greatly, I met my friend. For some moments we forgot even the severity of our sentence, conscious only of each other's presence.

But I soon turned from my friend to perform a more serious duty—that of writing to my father. I was desirous that the first tidings of my sad lot should reach my family from myself; in order that the grief which I knew they would all feel might be at least mitigated by hearing my state of mind, and the sentiments of peace and religion by which I was supported. The judges had given me a promise to expedite the letter the moment it was written.

Maroncelli next spoke to me respecting his trial; I acquainted him with mine, and we mutually described our prison walks and adventures, complimenting each other on our peripatetic philosophy. We approached our window, and saluted three of our friends, whom we beheld standing at theirs. Two of these were Canova and Rezia, in the same apartment; the first of whom was condemned to six years' hard imprisonment, and the last to three. The third was Doctor Cesare Armari, who had been my neighbour some preceding months, in the prisons of the Piombi. He was not, however, among the condemned, and soon obtained his liberty.

The power of communicating with one or other of our fellow-prisoners, at all hours, was a great relief to our feelings. But when buried in silence and darkness, I was unable to compose myself to rest; I felt my head burn, and my heart bleed, as my thoughts reverted to home. Would my aged parents be enabled to bear up against so heavy a misfortune? would they find a sufficient resource in their other children? They were equally attached to all, and I valued myself least of all in that family of love: but will a father and a mother ever find in the children that remain to them a compensation for the one of whom they are deprived.

Had I dwelt only upon my relatives and a few other dear friends, much as I regretted them, my thoughts would have been less bitter than they were. But I thought of the insulting smile of that judge, of the trial, the cause of the respective sentences, political passions and enmities, and the fate of so many of my friends, ... It was then I could no longer think with patience or indulgence of any of my persecutors. God had subjected me to a severe trial, and it was my duty to have borne it with courage. Alas! I was neither able nor willing. The pride and luxury of hatred pleased me better than the noble spirit of forgiveness; and I passed a night of horror after receiving sentence.

In the morning I could not pray. The universe appeared to me, then, to be the work of some power, the enemy of good. I had previously, indeed, been guilty of calumniating my Creator; but little did I imagine I should revert to such ingratitude, and in so brief a time. Julian, in his most impious moods, could not express himself more impiously than myself. To gloat over thoughts of hatred, or fierce revenge, when smarting under the scourge of heaviest calamity, instead of flying to religion as a refuge, renders a man criminal, even though his cause be just.. If we hate, it is a proof of rank pride; and where is the wretched mortal that dare stand up and declare in the face of Heaven, his title to hatred and revenge against his fellows? to assert that none have a right to sit in judgment upon him and his actions;—that none can injure him without a bad intention, or a violation of all justice? In short, he dares to arraign the decrees of Heaven itself, if it please Providence to make him suffer in a manner which he does not himself approve.

Still I was unhappy because I could not pray; for when pride reigns supreme, it acknowledges no other god than the self-idol it has created. How I could have wished to recommend to the Supreme Protector, the care of my bereaved parents, though at that unhappy moment I felt as if I no more believed in Him.

CHAPTER LIII.

At nine in the morning Maroncelli and I were conducted into the gondola which conveyed us into the city. We alighted at the palace of the Doge, and proceeded to the prisons. We were placed in the apartment which had been occupied by Signor Caporali a few days before, but with whose fate we were not acquainted. Nine or ten sbirri were placed over us as a guard, and walking about, we awaited the moment of being brought into the square. There was considerable delay. The Inquisitor did not make his appearance till noon, and then informed us that it was time to go. The physician, also, presented himself, and advised us to take a small glass of mint-water, which we accepted on account of the extreme compassion which the good old man expressed for us. It was Dr. Dosmo. The head bailiff then advanced and fixed the hand-cuffs upon us. We followed him, accompanied by the other bailiffs.

We next descended the magnificent staircase of the Giganti, and we called to mind the old Doge Faliero, who was beheaded there. We entered through the great gate which opens upon the small square from the court-yard of the palace, and we then turned to the left, in the direction of the lake. In the centre of the small square was raised the scaffold which we were to ascend. From the staircase of the Giganti, extending to the scaffold, were two lines of Austrian soldiers, through which we passed.

After ascending the platform, we looked around us, and

saw an immense assembly of people, apparently struck with terror. In other directions were seen bands of armed men, to awe the multitude; and we were told that cannon were loaded in readiness to be discharged at a moment's notice. I was now exactly in the spot where, in September, 1820, just a month previous to my arrest, a mendicant had observed to me, "This is a place of misfortune."

I called to mind the circumstance, and reflected that very possibly in that immense throng of spectators the same person might be present, and perhaps even recognise me.

The German Captain now called out to us to turn towards the palace, and look up; we did so, and beheld, upon the lodge, a messenger of the Council, with a letter in his hand; it was the sentence; he began to read it in a loud voice.

It was ushered in by solemn silence, which was continued until he came to the words, *Condemned to death.* There was then heard one general murmur of compassion. This was followed by a similar silence, in order to hear the rest of the document. A fresh murmur arose on the announcement of the following:—condemned to hard imprisonment, Maroncelli for *twenty years*, and Pellico for *fifteen.*

The Captain made a sign for us to descend. We cast one glance around us, and came down. We re-entered the court-yard, mounted the great staircase, and were conducted into the room from which we had been dragged. The manacles were removed, and we were soon reconducted to San Michele.

CHAPTER LIV.

The prisoners who had been condemned before us had already set out for Lubiana and Spielberg, accompanied by a commissary of police. He was now expected back, in order to conduct us to our destination; but the interval of a month elapsed.

My time was chiefly spent in talking, and listening to the

conversation of others, in order to distract my attention. Maroncelli read me some of his literary productions, and in turn, I read him mine. One evening I read from the window my play of *Ester d'Engaddi*, to Canova, Rezia, and Armari; and the following evening, the *Iginia d'Asti*. During the night, however, I grew irritable and wretched, and was unable to sleep. I both desired and feared to learn in what manner the tidings of my calamity had been received by my family.

At length I got a letter from my father, and was grieved to find, from the date, that my last to him had not been sent, as I had requested of the Inquisitor, immediately! Thus my unhappy father, while flattering himself that I should be set at liberty, happening to take up the Milan Gazette, read the horrid sentence which I had just received upon the scaffold. He himself acquainted me with this fact, and left me to infer what his feelings must have been on meeting thus suddenly with the sad news. I cannot express the contempt and anger I felt on learning that my letter had been kept back; and how deeply I felt for all my poor unhappy family. There was doubtless no malice in this delay, but I looked upon it as a refinement of the most atrocious barbarity; an eager, infernal desire to see the iron enter, as it were, the very soul of my beloved and innocent relatives. I felt, indeed, as if I could have delighted to shed a sea of blood, could I only punish this flagrant and premeditated inhumanity.

Now that I judge calmly, I find it very improbable. The delay, doubtless, was simply owing to inadvertency on the part of subordinate agents. Enraged as I was, I heard with still more excited feelings that my companions were about to celebrate Easter week ere their departure. As for me, I considered it wholly impossible, inasmuch as I felt not the least disposition towards forgiveness. Should I be guilty of such a scandal!

CHAPTER LV.

At length the German commissioner arrived, and came to acquaint us that within two days we were to set out. "I have the pleasure," he added, "to give you some consoling tidings. On my return from Spielberg, I saw his majesty the Emperor at Vienna, who acquainted me that the penal days appointed you will not extend to twenty-four hours, but only to twelve. By this expression it is intended to signify that the pain will be divided, or half the punishment remitted." This division was never notified to us in an official form, but there is no reason to suppose that the commissioner would state an untruth; the less so as he made no secret of the information, which was known to the whole commission. Nevertheless, I could not congratulate myself upon it. To my feelings, seven years and a half had little more horrible in them (to be spent in chains and solitude) than fifteen; for I conceived it to be impossible to survive so long a period. My health had recently again become wretched! I suffered from severe pains of the chest, attended with cough, and thought my lungs were affected. I ate little, and that little I could not digest. Our departure took place on the night of the 25th of March. We were permitted to take leave of our friend, Cesare Armari. A sbirro chained us in a transverse manner, namely, the right hand and the left foot, so as to render it impossible for us to escape.

We went into a gondola, and the guards rowed us towards Fusina. On our arrival we found two boats in readiness for us. Rezia and Canova were placed in one, and Maroncelli and myself in the other. The commissary was also with two of the prisoners, and an under-commissary with the others. Six or seven guards of police completed our convoy; they were armed with swords and muskets; some of them at hand in the boats, others in the box of the Vetturino.

To be compelled by misfortune to leave one's country is always sufficiently painful; but to be torn from it in chains, doomed to exile in a horrible climate, to linger days, and hours, and years, in solitary dungeons, is a fate so appalling as to defy language to convey the remotest idea of it.

Ere we had traversed the Alps, I felt that my country was becoming doubly dear to me; the sympathy we awakened on every side, from all ranks, formed an irresistible appeal to my affection and gratitude. In every city, in every village, in every group of meanest houses, the news of our condemnation had been known for some weeks, and we were expected. In several places the commissioners and the guards had difficulty in dispersing the crowd which surrounded us. It was astonishing to witness the benevolent and humane feeling generally manifested in our behalf.

In Udine we met with a singular and touching incident. On arriving at the inn, the commissary caused the door of the court-yard to be closed, in order to keep back the people. A room was assigned us, and he ordered the waiters to bring supper, and make such accommodation as we required for repose. In a few moments three men entered with mattresses upon their shoulders. What was our surprise to see that only one of them was a servant of the inn; the other two were our acquaintance. We pretended to assist them in placing the beds, and had time to recognise and give each other the hand of fellowship and sympathy. It was too much; the tears started to our eyes. Ah! how trying was it to us all, not to be allowed the sad satisfaction even of shedding them in a last embrace.

The commissaries were not aware of the circumstance; but I had reason to think that one of the guards saw into the affair, just as the good Dario grasped me by the hand. He was a Venetian; he fixed his eyes upon us both; he turned pale; appeared in the act of making an alarm, then turned away his eyes, as if pretending not to see us. If he felt not assured that they were indeed our friends, he must have believed them to be some waiters with whom we were acquainted.

CHAPTER LVI.

The next morning we left Udine by dawn of day. The affectionate Dario was already in the street, wrapped in his mantle; he beckoned to us and followed us a long way. A coach also continued at some little distance from us for several miles. Some one waved a handkerchief from it, till it turned back; who could it have been? We had our own conjectures on the subject. May Heaven protect those generous spirits that thus cease not to love, and express their love for the unfortunate. I had the more reason to prize them from the fact of having met with cowards, who, not content with denying me, thought to benefit themselves by calumniating their once fortunate *friend*. These cases, however, were rare, while those of the former, to the honour of the human character, were numerous.

I had supposed that the warm sympathy expressed for us in Italy would cease when we entered on a foreign soil. But I was deceived; the good man is ever the fellow-countryman of the unhappy! When traversing Illyrian and German ground, it was the same as in our own country. There was the same general lamentation at our fate; "Arme herren!" poor gentlemen, was on the lips of all.

Sometimes, on entering another district, our escort was compelled to stop in order to decide in what part to take up our quarters. The people would then gather round us, and we heard exclamations, and other expressions of commiseration, which evidently came from the heart. These proofs of popular feeling were still more gratifying to me, than such as I had met with from my own countrymen. The consolation which was thus afforded me, helped to soothe the bitter indignation I then felt against those whom I esteemed my enemies. Yet, possibly, I reflected, if we were brought more nearly acquainted, if I could see into their real motives, and I could explain my own feelings, I might be constrained to admit that they are not impelled by the malignant spirit I suppose, while they would find there was as little of bad in me. Nay, they might perhaps be induced not only to pity, but to admire and love us!

It is true, indeed, that men too often hate each other, merely because they are strangers to each other's real views and feelings; and the simple interchange of a few words would make them acknowledge their error, and give the hand of brotherhood to each other.

We remained a day at Lubiana; and there Canova and Rezia were separated from us, being forthwith conducted into the castle. It is easy to guess our feelings upon this painful occasion.

On the evening of our arrival at Lubiana and the day following, a gentleman came and joined us, who, if I remember rightly, announced himself as the municipal secretary. His manners were gentle and humane, and he spoke of religion in a tone at once elevated and impressive. I conjectured he must be a priest, the priests in Germany being accustomed to dress exactly in the same style as laymen. His countenance was calculated to excite esteem. I regretted that I was not enabled further to cultivate his acquaintance, and I blame myself for my inadvertency in not having taken down his name.

It irks me, too, that I cannot at this time recall the name of another gentle being, a young girl of Styria, who followed us through the crowd, and when our coach stopped for a few minutes, moved towards us with both hands, and afterwards turned weeping away, supported by a young man, whose light hair proclaimed him of German extraction. But most probably he had been in Italy, where he had fallen in love with our fair countrywoman, and felt touched for our country. Yes! what pleasure it would have given me to record the names of those venerable fathers and mothers of families, who, in different districts, accosted us on our road, inquiring if we had parents and friends; and on hearing that we had, would grow pale, and exclaim, "Alas! may it please God to restore you soon to those wretched, bereaved ones whom you have left behind."

CHAPTER LVII.

ON the 10th of April we arrived at our place of destination.

The city of Brünn is the capital of Moravia, where the governor of the two provinces of Moravia and Silesia is accustomed to reside. Situated in a pleasant valley, it presents a rich and noble aspect. At one time it was a great manufactory of cloth, but its prosperous days were now passed, and its population did not exceed thirty thousand.

Contiguous to the walls on the western side rises a mount, and on this is placed the dreaded fortress of Spielberg, once the royal seat of the lords of Moravia, and now the most terrific prison under the Austrian monarchy. It was a well-guarded citadel, but was bombarded and taken by the French after the celebrated battle of Austerlitz, a village at a little distance from it. It was not generally repaired, with the exception of a portion of the outworks, which had been wholly demolished. Within it are imprisoned some three hundred wretches, for the most part robbers and assassins, some condemned to the *carcere duro*, others to that called *durissimo*, the severest of all. This HARD IMPRISONMENT comprehends compulsory, daily labour, to wear chains on the legs, to sleep upon bare boards, and to eat the worst imaginable food. The *durissimo*, or hardest, signifies being chained in a more horrible manner, one part of the iron being fixed in the wall, united to a hoop round tho body of the prisoner, so as to prevent his moving further than the board which serves for his couch. We, as state prisoners, were condemned to the *carcere duro.* The food, however, is the same, though in the words of the law it is prescribed to be bread and water.

While mounting the acclivity we turned our eyes as if to take a last look of the world we were leaving, doubting if ever the portals of that living grave would be again unclosed to us. I was calm, but rage and indignation consumed my heart. It was in vain I had recourse to philosophy; it had no arguments to quiet or to support me.

I was in poor health on leaving Venice, and the journey had fatigued me exceedingly. I had a fever, and felt severe pains, both in my head and my limbs. Illness increased my irritation, and very probably the last had an equally ill effect upon my frame.

We were consigned over to the superintendent of Spielberg, and our names were registered in the same list as that of the robbers. The imperial commissary shook our hands upon taking leave, and was evidently affected. "Farewell," he said, "and let me recommend to you calmness and submission: for I assure you the least infraction of discipline will be punished by the governor in the severest manner."

The consignment being made out, my friend and myself were conducted into a subterranean gallery, where two dismal-looking dungeons were unlocked, at a distance from each other. In one of these I was entombed alive, and poor Maroncelli in the other.

CHAPTER LVIII.

How bitter is it, after having bid adieu to so many beloved objects, and there remains only a single one between yourself and utter solitude, the solitude of chains and a living death, to be separated even from that one! Maroncelli, on leaving me, ill and dejected, shed tears over me as one whom, it was most probable, he would never more behold. In him, too, I lamented a noble-minded man, cut off in the splendour of his intellect, and the vigour of his days, snatched from society, all its duties and its pleasures, and even from "the common air, the earth, the sky." Yet he survived the unheard of afflictions heaped upon him, but in what a state did he leave his living tomb!

When I found myself alone in that horrid cavern, heard the closing of the iron doors, the rattling of chains, and by the gloomy light of a high window, saw the wooden bench destined for my couch, with an enormous chain fixed in the wall, I sat down, in sullen rage, on my hard resting-place, and taking up the chain, measured its length, in the belief that it was destined for me.

In half an hour I caught the sound of locks and keys; the door opened, and the head-jailer handed me a jug of water.

"Here is something to drink," he said in a rough tone, "and you will have your loaf to-morrow."

"Thanks, my good man."

"I am not good," was the reply.

"The worse for you," I answered, rather sharply. "And this great chain," I added, "is it for me?"

"It is, Sir; if you don't happen to be quiet; if you get into a rage, or say impertinent things. But if you are reasonable, we shall only chain you by the feet. The blacksmith is getting all ready."

He then walked sullenly up and down, shaking that horrid ring of enormous keys, while with angry eye I measured his gigantic, lean, and aged figure. His features, though not decidedly vulgar, bore the most repulsive expression of brutal severity which I ever beheld!

How unjust are mankind when they presume to judge by

appearances, and in deference to their vain, arrogant prejudices. The man whom I upbraided in my heart for shaking as it were in triumph those horrible keys, to make me more keenly sensible of his power, whom I set down as an insignificant tyrant, inured to practices of cruelty, was then revolving thoughts of compassion, and assuredly had spoken in that harsh tone only to conceal his real feelings. Perhaps he was afraid to trust himself, or that I should prove unworthy gentler treatment; doubtful whether I might not be yet more criminal than unhappy, though willing to afford me relief.

Annoyed by his presence, and the sort of lordly air he assumed, I determined to try to humble him, and called out as if speaking to a servant, "Give me something to drink!" He looked at me, as much as to say, "Arrogant man! this is no place for you to show the airs of a master." Still he was silent, bent his long back, took up the jug, and gave it to me. I perceived, as I took it from him, that he trembled, and believing it to proceed from age, I felt a mingled emotion of reverence and compassion. "How old are you?" I inquired in a kinder tone.

"Seventy-four, Sir; I have lived to see great calamities, both as regards others and myself."

The tremulous emotion I had observed increased as he said this, and again took the jug from my hand. I now thought it might be owing to some nobler feeling than the effect of age, and the aversion I had conceived instantaneously left me.

"And what is your name?" I inquired.

"It pleased fortune, Sir, to make a fool of me, by giving me the name of a great man. My name is Schiller." He then told me in a few words, some particulars as to his native place, his family, the campaigns in which he had served, and the wounds he had received.

He was a Switzer, the son of peasants, had been in the

wars against the Turks, under Marshal Laudon, in the reign of Maria Theresa and Joseph II. He had subsequently served in the Austrian campaigns against France, up to the period of Napoleon's exile.

CHAPTER LIX.

When we begin to form a better opinion of one against whom we had conceived a strong prejudice, we seem to discover in every feature, in his voice, and manner, fresh marks of a good disposition, to which we were before strangers. Is this real, or is it not rather founded upon illusion? Shortly before, we interpreted the very same expressions in another way. Our judgment of moral qualities has undergone a change, and soon, the conclusions drawn from our knowledge of physiognomy are equally different. How many portraits of celebrated men inspire us only with respect or admiration because we know their characters; portraits which we should have pronounced worthless and unattractive had they represented the ordinary race of mortals. And thus it is, if we reason *vice versâ.* I once laughed, I remember, at a lady, who on beholding a likeness of Catiline mistook it for that of Collatinus, and remarked upon the sublime expression of grief in the features of Collatinus for the loss of his Lucretia. These sort of illusions are not uncommon. I would not maintain that the features of good men do not bear the impression of their character, like irreclaimable villains that of their depravity; but that there are many which have at least a doubtful cast. In short, I won a little upon old Schiller; I looked at him more attentively, and he no longer appeared forbidding. To say the truth, there was something in his language which, spite of its rough tone, showed the genuine traits of a noble mind. And spite of our first looks of mutual distrust and defiance, we seemed to feel a certain respect for each other; he spoke boldly what he thought, and so did I.

"Captain as I am," he observed, "I have fallen,—to take my rest, into this wretched post of jailer; and God knows it is far more disagreeable for me to maintain it, than it was to risk my life in battle."

I was now sorry I had asked him so haughtily to give me drink. "My dear Schiller," I said, grasping his hand, "it is in vain you deny it, I know you are a good fellow; and as I have fallen into this calamity, I thank heaven which has given me you for a guardian!"

He listened to me, shook his head, and then rubbing his forehead, like a man in some perplexity or trouble.

"No, Sir, I am bad—rank bad. They made me take an oath, which I must, and will keep. I am bound to treat all the prisoners, without distinction, with equal severity; no indulgence, no permission to relent, to soften the sternest orders, in particular as regards prisoners of state."

"You are a noble fellow; I respect you for making your duty a point of conscience. You may err, humanly speaking, but your motives are pure in the eyes of God."

"Poor gentleman, have patience, and pity me. I shall be hard as steel in my duty, but my heart bleeds to be unable to relieve the unfortunate. This is all I really wished to say." We were both affected.

He then entreated that I would preserve my calmness, and not give way to passion, as is too frequent with solitary prisoners, and calls for restraint, and even for severer punishment.

He afterwards resumed his gruff, affected tone as if to conceal the compassion he felt for me, observing that it was high time for him to go.

He came back, however, and inquired how long a time I had been afflicted with that horrible cough, reflecting sharply upon the physician for not coming to see me that very evening. "You are ill of a horse fever," he added, "I know it well; you will stand in need of a straw bed, but we cannot give you one till the doctor has ordered it."

He retired, locked the door, and I threw myself upon the hard boards, with considerable fever and pain in my chest, but less irritable, less at enmity with mankind, and less alienated from God.

CHAPTER LX.

In the evening came the superintendent, attended by Schiller, another captain, and two soldiers, to make the usual search. Three of these inquisitions were ordered each day, at morning, noon, and midnight. Every corner of the prison was examined, and each article of the most trivial kind. The inferior officers then left, and the superintendent remained a little time to converse with me.

The first time I saw this troop of jailers approach, a strange thought came into my head. Being unacquainted with their habits of search, and half delirious with fever, it struck me that they were come to take my life, and seizing my great chain I resolved to sell it dearly by knocking the first upon the head that offered to molest me.

"What mean you?" exclaimed the superintendent; "we are not going to hurt you. It is merely a formal visit to ascertain that all is in proper order in the prisons."

I hesitated, but when I saw Schiller advance and stretch forth his hand with a kind, paternal look, I dropped the chain and took his proffered hand. "Lord! how it burns," he said, turning towards the superintendent; "he ought at least to have a straw bed;" and he said this in so truly compassionate a tone as quite to win my heart. The superintendent then felt my pulse, and spoke some consolatory words: he was a man of gentlemanly manners, but dared not for his life express any opinion upon the subject,

"It is all a reign of terror here," said he, "even as

regards myself. Should I not execute my orders to the rigour of the letter, you would no longer see me here." Schiller made a long face, and I could have wagered he said within himself, "But if I were at the head, like you, I would not carry my apprehensions so very far; for to give an opinion on a matter of such evident necessity, and so innocuous to government, would never be esteemed a mighty fault."

When left alone, I felt my heart, so long incapable of any deep sense of religion, stirred within me, and knelt down to pray. I besought a blessing upon the head of old Schiller, and appealing to God, asked that he would so move the hearts of those around me, as to permit me to become attached to them, and no longer suffer me to hate my fellow-beings, humbly accepting all that was to be inflicted upon me from His hand.

About midnight I heard people passing along the gallery. Keys were sounding, and soon the door opened; it was the captain and his guards on search.

"Where is my old Schiller?" inquired I. He had stopped outside in the gallery.

"I am here—I am here!" was the answer. He came towards the table, and, feeling my pulse, hung over me as a father would over his child with anxious and inquiring look. "Now I remember," said he, "to-morrow is Thursday."

"And what of that?" I inquired.

"Why! it is just one of the days when the doctor does not attend, he comes only on a Monday, Wednesday, and Friday. Plague on him."

"Give yourself no uneasiness about that!"

"No uneasiness, no uneasiness!" he muttered, "but I do; you are ill, I see; nothing is talked of in the whole town but the arrival of yourself and friends; the doctor must have heard of it; and why the devil could he not make the extraordinary exertion of coming once out of his time?"

"Who knows!" said I, "he may perhaps be here to-morrow,—Thursday though it will be?"

The old man said no more, he gave me a squeeze of the hand, enough to break every bone in my fingers, as a mark of his approbation of my courage and resignation. I was a little angry with him, however, much as a young lover, if the girl of his heart happen in dancing to press her foot upon his; he laughs and esteems himself highly favoured, instead of crying out with the pain.

CHAPTER LXI.

I AWOKE on Thursday morning, after a horrible night, weak, aching in all my bones, from the hard boards, and in a profuse perspiration. The visit hour came, but the superintendent was absent; and he only followed at a more convenient time. I said to Schiller, "Just see how terribly I perspire; but it is now growing cold upon me; what a treat it would be to change my shirt."

"You cannot do it," he said, in a brutal tone. At the same time he winked, and moved his hand. The captain and guards withdrew, and Schiller made me another sign as he closed the door. He soon opened it again, and brought one of his own shirts, long enough to cover me from head to foot, even if doubled.

"It is perhaps a little too long, but I have no others here."

"I thank you, friend, but as I brought with me a whole trunk full of linen, I do hope I may be permitted the use of it. Have the kindness to ask the superintendent to let me have one of my shirts."

"You will not be permitted, Sir, to use any of your

linen here. Each week you will have a shirt given you from the house like the other prisoners."

"You see, good man, in what a condition I am. I shall never go out of here alive. I shall never be able to reward you."

"For shame, Sir! for shame!" said the old man. "Talk of reward to one who can do you no good! to one who dare hardly give a dry shirt to a sick fellow creature in a sweat!" He then helped me on with his long shirt, grumbling all the while, and slammed the door to with violence on going out, as if he had been in a great rage.

About two hours after, he brought me a piece of black bread. "This," he said, "is your two days' fare!" he then began to walk about in a sulky mood.

"What is the matter?" I inquired; "are you vexed at me? You know I took the shirt."

"I am enraged at that doctor; though it be Thursday he might show his ugly face here."

"Patience!" said I; but though I said it, I knew not for the life of me how to get the least rest, without a pillow, upon those hard boards. Every bone in my body suffered. At eleven I was treated to the prison dinner—two little iron pots, one of soup, the other of herbs, mixed in such a way as to turn your stomach with the smell. I tried to swallow a few spoonfuls, but did not succeed. Schiller encouraged me: "Never despair," said he; "try again; you will get used to it in time. If you don't, you will be like many others before you, unable to eat anything but bread, and die of mere inanition."

Friday morning came, and with it came Dr. Bayer at last. He found me very feverish, ordered me a straw bed, and insisted I should be removed from the caverns into one of the abodes above. It could not be done; there was no room. An appeal was made to the Governor of Moravia and Silesia, residing at Brünn, who commanded, on the urgency of the case, that the medical advice should be followed.

There was a little light in the room to which I was removed. I crawled towards the bars of the narrow window, and had the delight of seeing the valley that lay below,—part of the city of Brünn,—a suburb with gardens,—the churchyard,—the little lake of Certosa,—and the woody hills which lay between us and the famous plains of Austerlitz. I was enchanted, and oh, what double pleasure, thought I, would be mine, were I enabled to share it with my poor friend Maroncelli!

CHAPTER LXII.

MEANWHILE, our prison dresses were making for us, and five days afterwards mine was brought to me. It consisted of a pair of pantaloons made of rough cloth, of which the right side was grey, the left of a dark colour. The waistcoat was likewise of two colours equally divided, as well as the jacket, but with the same colours placed on the contrary sides. The stockings were of the coarsest wool; the shirt of linen tow full of sharp points—a true hair-cloth garment; and round the neck was a piece of the same kind. Our legs were enveloped in leather buskins, untanned, and we wore a coarse white hat.

This costume was not complete without the addition of chains to the feet, that is, extending from one leg to the other, the joints being fastened with nails, which were riveted upon an anvil. The blacksmith employed upon my legs, in this operation, observed to one of the guards, thinking I knew nothing of German, "So ill as he is, one would think they might spare him this sort of fun; ere two months be over, the angel of death will loosen these rivets of mine."

"*Möchte es seyn!* may it be so!" was my reply, as I

touched him upon the shoulder. The poor fellow started, and seemed quite confused; he then said; "I hope I may be a false prophet; and I wish you may be set free by another kind of angel."

"Yet, rather than live thus, think you not, it would be welcome even from the angel of death?" He nodded his head, and went away, with a look of deep compassion for me.

I would truly have been willing to die, but I felt no disposition towards suicide. I felt confident that the disease of my lungs would be enough, ere long, to give me freedom. Such was not the will of God. The fatigue of my journey had made me much worse, but rest seemed again to restore my powers.

A few minutes after the blacksmith left me, I heard the hammer sounding upon the anvil in one of the caverns below. Schiller was then in my room. "Do you hear those blows?" I said; "they are certainly fixing the irons on poor Maroncelli." The idea for the moment was so overwhelming, that if the old man had not caught me, I should have fallen. For more than half an hour, I continued in a kind of swoon, and yet I was sensible. I could not speak, my pulse scarcely beat at all; a cold sweat bathed me from head to foot. Still I could hear all that Schiller said, and had a keen perception, both of what had passed and was passing.

By command of the superintendent and the activity of the guards, the whole of the adjacent prisons had been kept in a state of profound silence. Three or four times I had caught snatches of some Italian song, but they were quickly stifled by the calls of the sentinels on duty. Several of these were stationed upon the ground-floor, under our windows, and one in the gallery close by, who was continually engaged in listening at the doors and looking through the bars to forbid every kind of noise.

Once, towards evening (I feel the same sort of emotion

whenever I recur to it), it happened that the sentinels were less on the alert; and I heard in a low but clear voice some one singing in a prison adjoining my own. What joy, what agitation I felt at the sound. I rose from my bed of straw, I bent my ear; and when it ceased—I burst into tears. "Who art thou, unhappy one?" I cried, "who art thou? tell me thy name! I am Silvio Pellico."

"Oh, Silvio!" cried my neighbour, "I know you not by person, but I have long loved you. Get up to your window, and let us speak to each other, in spite of the jailers."

I crawled up as well as I could; he told me his name, and we exchanged few words of kindness. It was the Count Antonio Oroboni, a native of Fratta, near Rovigo, and only twenty-nine years of age. Alas! we were soon interrupted by the ferocious cries of the sentinels. He in the gallery knocked as loud as he could with the butt-end of his musket, both at the Count's door and at mine. We would not, and we could not obey; but the noise, the oaths, and threats of the guards were such as to drown our voices, and after arranging that we would resume our communications, upon a change of guards, we ceased to converse.

CHAPTER LXIII.

We were in hopes (and so in fact it happened) that by speaking in a lower tone, and perhaps occasionally having guards whose humanity might prompt them to pay no attention to us, we might renew our conversation. By dint of practice we learnt to hear each other in so low a key that the sounds were almost sure to escape the notice of the sentinels. If, as it rarely happened, we forgot ourselves, and talked aloud, there came down upon us a torrent of cries, and knocks at our doors, accompanied with threats and curses of every kind, to say nothing of poor Schiller's vexation, and that of the superintendent.

By degrees, however, we brought our system to perfection; spoke only at the precise minutes, quarters, and half hours when it was safe, or when such and such guards were upon duty. At length, with moderate caution, we were enabled every day to converse almost as much as we pleased, without drawing on us the attention or anger of any of the superior officers.

It was thus we contracted an intimate friendship. The Count told me his adventures, and in turn I related mine. We sympathised in everything we heard, and in all each other's joys or griefs. It was of infinite advantage to us, as well as pleasure; for often, after passing a sleepless night, one or the other would hasten to the window and salute his friend. How these mutual welcomes and conversations helped to encourage us, and to soothe the horrors of our continued solitude! We felt that we were useful to each other; and the sense of this roused a gentle emulation in all our thoughts, and gave a satisfaction which man receives, even in misery, when he knows he can serve a fellow-creature. Each conversation gave rise to new ones; it was necessary to continue them, and to explain as we went on. It was an unceasing stimulus to our ideas, to our reason, our memory, our imagination, and our hearts.

At first, indeed, calling to mind Julian, I was doubtful as to the fidelity of this new friend. I reflected that hitherto we had not been at variance; but some day I feared something unpleasant might occur, and that I should then be sent back to my solitude. But this suspicion was soon removed. Our opinions harmonised upon all essential points. To a noble mind, full of ardour and generous sentiment, undaunted by misfortune, he added the most clear and perfect faith in Christianity, while in me this had become vacillating and at times apparently extinct.

He met my doubts with most just and admirable reflections; and with equal affection, I felt that he had reason on his side: I admitted it, yet still my doubts returned. It is thus, I believe, with all who have not the Gospel at heart, and who hate, or indulge resentments of any kind. The mind catches glimpses, as it were, of the truth, but as it is unpleasing, it is disbelieved the moment after, and the attention directed elsewhere.

Oroboni was indefatigable in turning *my* attention to the motives which man has to show kindness to his enemies. I never spoke of any one I abhorred but he began in a most dexterous manner to defend him, and not less by his words than by his example. Many men had injured him; it grieved him, yet he forgave all, and had the magnanimity to relate some laudable trait or other belonging to each, and seemed to do it with pleasure.

The irritation which had obtained such a mastery over me, and rendered me so irreligious after my condemnation, continued several weeks, and then wholly ceased. The noble virtue of Oroboni delighted me. Struggling as well as I could to reach him, I at least trod in the same track, and I was then enabled to pray with sincerity; to forgive, to hate no one, and dissipate every remaining doubt and gloom.

*Ubi charitas et amor, Deus ibi est.**

CHAPTER LXIV.

To say truth, if our punishment was excessively severe, and calculated to irritate the mind, we had still the rare fortune of meeting only with individuals of real worth. They could not, indeed, alleviate our situation, except by kindness and respect, but so much was freely granted. If there were something rude and uncouth in old Schiller, it was amply compensated by his noble spirit. Even the wretched Kunda (the convict who brought us our dinner, and water three times a-day) was anxious to show his compassion for

* Where charity and love are, God is present.

us. He swept our rooms regularly twice in the week. One morning, while thus engaged, as Schiller turned a few steps from the door, poor Kunda offered me a piece of white bread. I refused it, but squeezed him cordially by the hand. He was moved, and told me, in bad German, that he was a Pole. "Good sir," he added, "they give us so little to eat here, that I am sure you must be hungry." I assured him I was not, but he was very hard of belief.

The physician, perceiving that we were none of us enabled to swallow the kind of food prepared for us on our first arrival, put us all upon what is considered the hospital diet. This consisted of three very small plates of soup in the day, the least slice of roast lamb, hardly a mouthful, and about three ounces of white bread.

As my health continued to improve, my appetite grew better, and that "fourth portion," as they termed it, was really too little, and I began to feel the justice of poor Kunda's remarks. I tried a return to the sound diet, but do what I would to conquer my aversion, it was all labour lost. I was compelled to live upon the fourth part of ordinary meals: and for a whole year I knew by experience the tortures of hunger. It was still more severely felt by many of my fellow-prisoners, who, being far stouter, had been accustomed to a full and generous diet. I learnt that many of them were glad to accept pieces of bread from Schiller and some of the guards, and even from the poor hungry Kunda.

"It is reported in the city," said the barber, a young practitioner of our surgery, one day to me, "it is reported that they do not give you gentlemen here enough to eat."

"And it is very true," replied I, with perfect sincerity.

The next Sunday (he came always on that day) he brought me an immense white loaf, and Schiller pretended not to see him give it me. Had I listened to my stomach I should have accepted it, but I would not, lest he should repeat the gift and bring himself into some trouble. For the same reason I refused Schiller's offers. He would often bring me boiled meat, entreating me to partake of it, and protesting it cost him nothing; besides, he knew not what to do with it, and must give it away to somebody. I could have devoured it, but would he not then be tempted to offer me something or other every day, and what would it end in? Twice only I partook of some cherries and some pears; they were quite irresistible. I was punished as I expected, for from that time forth the old man never ceased bringing me fruit of some kind or other.

CHAPTER LXV.

It was arranged, on our arrival, that each of us should be permitted to walk an hour twice in the week. In the sequel, this relief was one day granted us and another refused; and the hour was always later during festivals.

We went, each separately, between two guards, with loaded muskets on their shoulders. In passing from my prison, at the head of the gallery, I went by the whole of the Italian prisoners, with the exception of Maroncelli—the only one condemned to linger in the caverns below. "A pleasant walk!" whispered they all, as they saw me pass; but I was not allowed to exchange a single word.

I was led down a staircase which opened into a spacious court, where we walked upon a terrace, with a south aspect, and a view of the city of Brünn and the surrounding country. In this courtyard we saw numbers of the common criminals, coming from, or going to, their labour, or passing along conversing in groups. Among them were several Italian robbers, who saluted me with great respect. "He is no rogue, like us; yet you see his punishment is more severe"; and it was true, they had a larger share of freedom than I.

Upon hearing expressions like these, I turned and saluted them with a good-natured look. One of them observed, "It does me good to see you, sir, when you notice me. Possibly you may see something in my look not so very wicked. An unhappy passion instigated me to commit a crime, but believe me, sir, I am no villain!"

Saying this he burst into tears. I gave him my hand, but he was unable to return the pressure. At that moment, my guard, according to their instructions, drove him away, declaring that they must permit no one to approach me. The observations subsequently addressed to me were pretended to be spoken among each other; and if my two attendants became aware of it, they quickly interposed silence.

Prisoners of various ranks, and visitors of the superintendent, the chaplain, the sergeant, or some of the captains, were likewise to be seen there. "That is an Italian, that is an Italian!" they often whispered each other. They stopped to look at me, and they would say in German, supposing I should not understand them, "That poor gentleman will not live to be old; he has death in his countenance."

In fact, after recovering some degree of strength, I again fell ill for want of nourishment, and fever again attacked me. I attempted to drag myself, as far as my chain would permit, along the walk, and throwing myself upon the turf, I rested there until the expiration of my hour. The guards would then sit down near me, and begin to converse with each other. One of them, a Bohemian, named Kral, had, though very poor, received some sort of an education, which he had himself improved by reflection. He was fond of reading, had studied Klopstock, Wieland, Goethe, Schiller, and many other distinguished German writers. He knew a good deal by memory, and repeated many passages with feeling and correctness. The other guard was a Pole, by name Kubitzky, wholly untaught, but kind and respectful. Their society was a great relief to me.

CHAPTER LXVI.

At one end of the terrace was situated the apartments of the superintendent, at the other was the residence of a captain, with his wife and son. When I saw any one appear from these buildings, I was in the habit of approaching near, and was invariably received with marks of courtesy and compassion.

The wife of the captain had been long ill, and appeared to be in a decline. She was sometimes carried into the open air, and it was astonishing to see the sympathy she expressed for our sufferings. She had the sweetest look I ever saw; and though evidently timid, would at times fix her eye upon me with an inquiring, confiding glance, when appealed to by name. One day I observed to her with a smile, "Do you know, signora, I find a resemblance between you and one who was very dear to me." She blushed, and replied with charming simplicity, "Do not then forget me when I shall be no more; pray for my unhappy soul, and for the little ones I leave behind me!" I never saw her after that day; she was unable to rise from her bed, and in a few months I heard of her death.

She left three sons, all beautiful as cherubs, and one still an infant at the breast. I had often seen the poor mother embrace them when I was by, and say, with tears in her eyes, "Who will be their mother when I am gone? Ah, whoever she may be, may it please the Father of all to inspire her with love, even for children not her own."

Often, when she was no more, did I embrace those fair children, shed a tear over them, and invoke their mother's blessing on them, in the same words. Thoughts of my own mother, and of the prayers she so often offered up for *her* lost son, would then come over me, and I added, with broken words and sighs, "Oh, happier mother than mine, you left, indeed, these innocent ones, so young and fair, but my dear mother devoted long years of care and tenderness to me, and saw them all, with the object of them, snatched from her at a blow!"

These children were intrusted to the care of two elderly and excellent women; one of them the mother, the other the aunt of the superintendent. They wished to hear the whole of my history, and I gave it them as briefly as I could. "How greatly we regret," they observed, with warm sympathy, "to be unable to help you in any way. Be assured, however, we offer up constant prayers for you, and if ever the day come that brings you liberty, it will be celebrated by all our family, like one of the happiest festivals."

The first-mentioned of these ladies had a remarkably sweet and soothing voice, united to an eloquence rarely to be heard from the lips of woman. I listened to her religious exhortations with a feeling of filial gratitude, and they sunk deep into my heart. Though her observations were not new to me, they were always applicable, and most valuable to me, as will appear from what follows:

"Misfortune cannot degrade a man, unless he be intrinsically mean; it rather elevates him.——"If we could penetrate the judgments of God, we should find that frequently the objects most to be pitied were the conquerors, not the conquered; the joyous rather than the sorrowful; the wealthy rather than those who are despoiled of all."——"The particular kindness shown by the Saviour of mankind to the unfortunate is a striking fact."——"That man ought to feel honoured in bearing the cross, when he considers that it was borne up the mount of our redemption by the Divinity himself in human form."

Such were among the excellent sentiments she inculcated;

but it was my lot, as usual, to lose these delightful friends when I had become most attached to them. They removed from the castle, and the sweet children no longer made their appearance upon the terrace. I felt this double deprivation more than I can express.

CHAPTER LXVII.

THE inconvenience I experienced from the chain upon my legs, which prevented me from sleeping, destroyed my health. Schiller wished me to petition, declaring that it was the duty of the physician to order it to be taken off. For some time I refused to listen to him, I then yielded, and informed the doctor that, in order to obtain a little sleep, I should be thankful to have the chain removed, if only for a few days. He answered that my fever was not yet so bad as to require it; and that it was necessary I should become accustomed to the chain. I felt indignant at this reply, and more so at myself for having asked the favour. "See what I have got by following your advice," said I to Schiller; and I said it in a very sharp tone, not a little offensive to the old man.

"You are vexed," he exclaimed, "because you met with a denial; and I am as much so with your arrogance! Could I help it?" He then began a long sermon. "The proud value themselves mightily in never exposing themselves to a refusal, in never accepting an offer, in being ashamed at a thousand little matters. *Alle eselen*, asses as they all are. Vain grandeur, want of true dignity, which consists in being ashamed only of bad actions!" He went off, and made the door ring with a tremendous noise.

I was dismayed; yet his rough sincerity scarcely displeased me. Had he not spoken the truth? to how many weaknesses had I not given the name of dignity! the result of nothing but pride.

At the dinner hour Schiller left my fare to the convict Kunda, who brought me some water, while Schiller stood outside. I called him. "I have no time," he replied, very drily.

I rose, and going to him, said, "If you wish my dinner to agree with me, pray don't look so horribly sour; it is worse than vinegar."

"And how ought I to look?" he asked, rather more appeased.

"Cheerful, and like a friend," was my reply. .

"Let us be merry, then! *Viva l'allegria!*" cried the old man. "And if it will make your dinner agree with you, I will dance you a hornpipe into the bargain." And, assuming a broad grin, he set to work with his long, lean, spindle shanks, which he worked about like two huge stilts, till I thought I should have died with laughing. I laughed and almost cried at the same time.

CHAPTER LXVIII.

One evening Count Oroboni and I were standing at our windows complaining of the low diet to which we were subjected. Animated by the subject, we talked a little too loud, and the sentinels began to upbraid us. The superintendent, indeed, called in a loud voice to Schiller, as he happened to be passing, inquiring in a threatening voice why he did not keep a better watch, and teach us to be silent? Schiller came in a great rage to complain of me, and ordered me never more to think of speaking from the window. He wished me to promise that I would not.

"No!" replied I; "I shall do no such thing."

"Oh, *der Teufel; der Teufel!*"* exclaimed the old man; "do you say that to me? Have I not had a horrible strapping on your account?"

* The Devil! the Devil!

"I am sorry, dear Schiller, if you have suffered on my account. But I cannot promise what I do not mean to perform."

"And why not perform it?"

"Because I cannot; because this continual solitude is such a torment to me. No! I will speak as long as I have breath, and invite my neighbour to talk to me. If he refuse I will talk to my window-bars, I will talk to the hills before me, I will talk to the birds as they fly about. I will talk!"

"*Der Teufel!* you will! You had better promise!"

"No, no, no! never!" I exclaimed.

He threw down his huge bunch of keys, and ran about, crying, "*Der Teufel! der Teufel!*" Then, all at once, he threw his long bony arms about my neck: "By ——, and you shall talk! Am I to cease to be a man because of this vile mob of keys? You are a gentleman, and I like your spirit! I know you will not promise. I would do the same in your place."

I picked up his keys and presented them to him. "These keys," said I, "are not so bad after all; they cannot turn an honest soldier, like you, into a villainous *sgherro*."

"Why, if I thought they could, I would hand them back to my superiors, and say, 'If you will give me no bread but the wages of a hangman, I will go and beg alms from door to door.'"

He took out his handkerchief, dried his eyes, and then, raising them, seemed to pray inwardly for some time. I, too, offered up my secret prayers for this good old man. He saw it, and took my hand with a look of grateful respect.

Upon leaving me he said, in a low voice, "When you speak with Count Oroboni, speak as I do now. You will do me a double kindness: I shall hear no more cruel threats of my lord superintendent, and by not allowing any remarks of yours to be repeated in his ear, you will avoid giving fresh irritation to *one* who knows how to punish."

I assured him that not a word should come from either of our lips which could possibly give cause of offence. In fact, we required no further instructions to be cautious. Two prisoners desirous of communication are skilful enough to invent a language of their own, without the least danger of its being interpreted by any listener.

CHAPTER LXIX.

I HAD just been taking my morning's walk; it was the 7th of August. Oroboni's dungeon door was standing open; Schiller was in it, and he was not sensible of my approach. My guards pressed forward in order to close my friend's door, but I was too quick for them; I darted into the room, and the next moment found myself in the arms of Count Oroboni.

Schiller was in dismay, and cried out "*Der Teufel! der Teufel!*" most vigorously, at the same time raising his finger in a threatening attitude. It was in vain, for his eyes filled with tears, and he cried out, sobbing, "Oh, my God! take pity on these poor young men and me; on all the unhappy like them, my God, who knows what it is to be so very unhappy upon earth!" The guards, also, both wept; the sentinel on duty in the gallery ran to the spot, and even he caught the infection.

"Silvio! Silvio!" exclaimed the Count, "this is the most delightful day of my life!" I know not how I answered him; I was nearly distracted with joy and affection.

When Schiller at length beseeched us to separate, and it was necessary we should obey, Oroboni burst into a flood of tears. "Are we never to see each other again upon earth?" he exclaimed, in a wild, prophetic tone.

Alas! I never saw him more! A very few months after

this parting, his dungeon was empty, and Oroboni lay at rest in the cemetery, on which I looked out from my window!

From the moment we had met, it seemed as if the tie which bound us were drawn closer round our hearts; and we were become still more necessary to each other.

He was a fine young man, with a noble countenance, but pale, and in poor health. Still, his eyes retained all their lustre. My affection for him was increased by a knowledge of his extreme weakness and sufferings. He felt for me in the same manner; we saw by how frail a tenure hung the lives of both, and that one must speedily be the survivor.

In a few days he became worse; I could only grieve and pray for him. After several feverish attacks, he recovered a little, and was even enabled to resume our conversations. What ineffable pleasure I experienced on hearing once more the sound of his voice! "You seem glad," he said, "but do not deceive yourself; it is but for a short time. Have the courage to prepare for my departure, and your virtuous resolution will inspire me also with courage!"

At this period the walls of our prison were about to be whitewashed, and meantime we were to take up our abode in the caverns below. Unfortunately they placed us in dungeons apart from each other. But Schiller told me that the Count was well; though I had my doubts, and dreaded lest his health should receive a last blow from the effects of his subterranean abode. If I had only had the good fortune, thought I, to be near my friend Maroncelli; I could distinguish his voice, however, as he sung. We spoke to each other, spite of the shouts and conversation of the guards. At the same period, the head physician of Brünn paid us a visit. He was sent in consequence of the report made by the superintendent in regard to the extreme ill health of the prisoners from the scanty allowance of food. A scorbutic epidemic was already fast emptying the dungeons. Not aware of the cause of his visit, I imagined that he came to see Oroboni, and my anxiety was inexpressible; I was bowed down with sorrow, and I too wished to die. The thought of suicide again tormented me. I struggled, indeed; but I felt like the weary traveller, who though compelled to press forward, feels an almost irresistible desire to throw himself upon the ground and rest.

I had been just informed that in one of those subterranean dens an aged Bohemian gentleman had recently destroyed himself by beating his head against the walls. I wish I had not heard it; for I could not, do what I would, banish the temptation to imitate him. It was a sort of delirium, and would most probably have ended in suicide, had not a violent gush of blood from my chest, which made me think that death was close at hand, relieved me. I was thankful to God that it should happen in this manner, and spare me an act of desperation, which my reason so strongly condemned. But Providence ordered it otherwise; I found myself considerably better after the discharge of blood from my lungs. Meantime, I was removed to the prison above, and the additional light, with the vicinity of my friend Oroboni, reconciled me to life.

CHAPTER LXX.

I FIRST informed the Count of the terrific melancholy I had endured when separated from him; and he declared he had been haunted with a similar temptation to suicide. "Let us take advantage," he said, "of the little time that remains for us, by mutually consoling each other. We will speak of God; emulate each other in loving him, and inculcate upon each other that he only is Justice, Wisdom, Goodness, Beauty — is all which is most worthy to be reverenced and adored. I tell you, friend, of a truth, that death is not far from me. I shall be eternally grateful,

Silvio, if you will help me, in these my last moments, to become as religious as I ought to have been during my whole life."

We now, therefore, confined our conversation wholly to religious subjects, especially to drawing parallels between the Christian philosophy and that of mere worldly founders of the Epicurean schools. We were both delighted to discover so strict an union between Christianity and reason; and both, on a comparison of the different evangelical communions, fully agreed that the catholic was the only one which could successfully resist the test of criticism,—which consisted of the purest doctrines and the purest morality—not of those wretched extremes, the product of human ignorance.

"And if by any unexpected accident," observed Oroboni, "we should be restored to society, should we be so mean-spirited as to shrink from confessing our faith in the Gospel? Should we stand firm if accused of having changed our sentiments in consequence of prison discipline?"

"Your question, my dear Oroboni," I replied, "acquaints me with the nature of your reply; it is also mine. The vilest servility is that of being subjected to the opinions of others, when we feel a persuasion at the same time that they are false. I cannot believe that either you or I could be guilty of so much meanness." During these confidential communications of our sentiments, I committed one fault. I had pledged my honour to Julian never to reveal, by mention of his real name, the correspondence which had passed between us. I informed poor Oroboni of it all, observing that "it never should escape my lips in any other place; but here we are immured as in a tomb; and even should you get free, I know I can confide in you as in myself."

My excellent friend returned no answer. "Why are you silent?" I enquired. He then seriously upbraided me for having broken my word and betrayed my friend's secret. His reproach was just; no friendship, however intimate, however fortified by virtue, can authorise such a violation of confidence, guaranteed, as it had been, by a sacred vow.

Since, however, it was done, Oroboni was desirous of turning my fault to a good account. He was acquainted with Julian, and related several traits of character, highly honourable to him. "Indeed," he added, "he has so often acted like a true Christian, that he will never carry his enmity to such a religion to the grave with him. Let us hope so; let us not cease to hope. And you, Silvio, try to pardon his ill-humour from your heart; and pray for him!" His words were held sacred by me.

CHAPTER LXXI.

The conversations of which I speak, sometimes with Oroboni, and sometimes with Schiller, occupied but a small portion of the twenty-four hours daily upon my hands. It was not always, moreover, that I could converse with Oroboni. How was I to pass the solitary hours? I was accustomed to rise at dawn, and mounting upon the top of my table, I grasped the bars of my window, and there said my prayers. The Count was already at his window, or speedily followed my example. We saluted each other, and continued for a time in secret prayer. Horrible as our dungeons were, they made us more truly sensible of the beauty of the world without, and the landscape that spread around us. The sky, the plains, the far off noise and motions of animals in the valley, the voices of the village maidens, the laugh, the song, had a charm for us it is difficult to express, and made us more dearly sensible of the presence of him who is so magnificent in his goodness, and of whom we ever stand in so much need.

The morning visit of the guards was devoted to an

examination of my dungeon, to see that all was in order. They felt at my chain, link by link, to be sure that no conspiracy was at work, or rather in obedience to the laws of discipline which bound them. If it were the day for the doctor's visit, Schiller was accustomed to ask us if we wished to see him, and to make a note to that effect.

The search being over, Schiller made his appearance, accompanied by Kunda, whose care it was to clean our rooms. Shortly after he brought our breakfast—a little pot of hogwash, and three small slices of coarse bread. The bread I was able to eat, but could not contrive to drink the swill.

It was next my business to apply to study. Maroncelli had brought a number of books from Italy, as well as some other of our fellow-prisoners—some more, and some less, but altogether they formed a pretty good library. This, too, we hoped to enlarge by some purchases; but awaited an answer from the Emperor, as to whether we might be permitted to read them and buy others. Meantime the governor gave us permission, *provisionally*, to have each two books at a time, and to exchange them when we pleased. About nine came the superintendent, and if the doctor had been summoned, he accompanied him.

I was allowed another interval for study between this and the dinner hour at eleven. We had then no further visits till sunset, and I returned to my studies. Schiller and Kunda then appeared with a change of water, and a moment afterwards, the superintendent with the guards to make their evening inspection, never forgetting my chain. Either before or after dinner, as best pleased the guards, we were permitted in turn to take our hour's walk. The evening search being over, Oroboni and I began our conversation,—always more extended than at any other hour. The other periods were, as related in the morning, or directly after dinner — but our words were then generally very brief. At times the sentinels were so kind as to say to us: "A little lower key, gentlemen, or otherwise the punishment will fall upon us." Not unfrequently they would pretend not to see us, and if the sergeant appeared, begged us to stop till he were past, when they told us we might talk again — "But as low as you possibly can, gentlemen, if you please!"

Nay, it happened that they would quietly accost us themselves; answer our questions, and give us some information respecting Italy.

Touching upon some topics, they entreated of us to be silent, refusing to give any answer. We were naturally doubtful whether these voluntary conversations, on their part, were really sincere, or the result of an artful attempt to pry into our secret opinions.

I am, however, inclined to think that they meant it all in good part, and spoke to us in perfect kindness and frankness of heart.

CHAPTER LXXII.

One evening the sentinels were more than usually kind and forbearing, and poor Oroboni and I conversed without in the least suppressing our voices. Maroncelli, in his subterraneous abode, caught the sound, and climbing up to the window, listened and distinguished my voice. He could not restrain his joy; but sung out my name, with a hearty welcome. He then asked me how I was, and expressed his regret that he had not yet been permitted to share the same dungeon. This favour I had, in fact, already petitioned for, but neither the superintendent nor the governor had the power of granting it. Our united wishes upon the same point had been represented to the Emperor, but no answer had hitherto been received by the governor of Brünn. Besides the instance in which we saluted each other in song, when in our subterraneous abodes, I had since heard the songs of the heroic Maroncelli, by fits and starts, in my dungeon above. He now raised his voice; he was no longer interrupted, and I caught all he said. I replied, and we continued the dialogue about a quarter of an hour Finally, they changed the sentinels upon the terrace, and the successors were not "of gentle mood." Often did we recommence the song, and as often were interrupted by furious cries, and curses, and threats, which we were compelled to obey.

Alas! my fancy often pictured to me the form of my friend, languishing in that dismal abode so much worse than my own; I thought of the bitter grief that must oppress him, and the effect upon his health, and bemoaned his fate in silence. Tears brought me no relief; the pains in my head returned, with acute fever. I could no longer stand, and took to my straw bed. Convulsions came on; the spasms in my breast were terrible. Of a truth, I believed that that night was my last.

The following day the fever ceased, my chest was relieved, but the inflammation seemed to have seized my brain, and I could not move my head without the most excruciating pain. I informed Oroboni of my condition, and he too was even worse than usual. "My dear friend," said he, "the day is near when one or other of us will no longer be able to reach the window. Each time we welcome one another may be the last. Let us hold ourselves in readiness, then, to die—yes to die! or to survive a friend." His voice trembled with emotion; I could not speak a word in reply. There was a pause, and he then resumed, "How fortunate you are in knowing the German language! You can at least have the advantage of a priest; I cannot obtain one acquainted with the Italian. But God is conscious of my wishes; I made confession at Venice—and in truth, it does not seem that I have met with anything since that loads my conscience."

"I, on the contrary, confessed at Venice," said I, "with my heart full of rancour, much worse than if I had wholly refused the sacrament. But if I could find a priest, I would now confess myself with all my heart, and pardon everybody, I can assure you."

"God bless you, Silvio!" he exclaimed, "you give me the greatest consolation I can receive. Yes, yes; dear friend! let us both do all in our power to merit a joyful meeting where we shall no more be separated, where we shall be united in happiness, as now we are in these last trying hours of our calamity."

The next day I expected him as usual at the window. But he came not, and I learnt from Schiller that he was grievously ill. In eight or ten days he recovered, and reappeared at his accustomed station. I complained to him bitterly, but he consoled me. A few months passed in this strange alternation of suffering; sometimes it was he, at others I, who was unable even to reach our window.

CHAPTER LXXIII.

I WAS enabled to keep up until the 11th of January, 1823. On that morning, I rose with a slight pain in my head, and a strong tendency to fainting. My legs trembled, and I could scarcely draw my breath.

Poor Oroboni, also, had been unable to rise from his straw for several days past. They brought me some soup, I took a spoonful, and then fell back in a swoon. Some time afterwards the sentinel in the gallery, happening to look through the pane of my door, saw me lying senseless on the ground, with the pot of soup at my side; and believing me to be dead, he called Schiller, who hastened, as well as the superintendent, to the spot.

The doctor was soon in attendance, and they put me on my bed. I was restored with great difficulty. Perceiving

I was in danger, the physician ordered my irons to be taken off. He then gave me some kind of cordial, but it would not stay on my stomach, while the pain in my head was horrible. A report was forthwith sent to the governor, who despatched a courier to Vienna, to ascertain in what manner I was to be treated. The answer received, was, that I should not be placed in the infirmary, but was to receive the same attendance in my dungeon as was customary in the former place. The superintendent was further authorised to supply me with soup from his own kitchen so long as I should continue unwell.

The last provision of the order received was wholly useless, as neither food nor beverage would stay on my stomach. I grew worse during a whole week, and was delirious without intermission, both day and night.

Kral and Kubitzky were appointed to take care of me, and both were exceedingly attentive. Whenever I showed the least return of reason, Kral was accustomed to say, "There! have faith in God; God alone is good."

"Pray for me," I stammered out, when a lucid interval first appeared: "pray for me not to live, but that he will accept my misfortunes and my death as an expiation." He suggested that I should take the sacrament.

"If I asked it not, attribute it to my poor head; it would be a great consolation to me."

Kral reported my words to the superintendent, and the chaplain of the prisons came to me. I made my confession, received the communion, and took the holy oil. The priest's name was Sturm, and I was satisfied with him. The reflections he made upon the justice of God, upon the injustice of man, upon the duty of forgiveness, and upon the vanity of all earthly things, were not out of place. They bore moreover the stamp of a dignified and well-cultivated mind as well as an ardent feeling of true love towards God and our neighbour.

CHAPTER LXXIV.

The exertion I made to receive the sacrament exhausted my remaining strength; but it was of use, as I fell into a deep sleep, which continued several hours.

On awaking I felt somewhat refreshed, and observing Schiller and Kral near me, I took them by the hand, and thanked them for their care. Schiller fixed his eyes on me.

"I am accustomed," he said, "to see persons at the last, and I would lay a wager that you will not die."

"Are you not giving me a bad prognostic?" said I.

"No;" he replied, "the miseries of life are great it is true; but he who supports them with dignity and with humility must always gain something by living." He then added, "If you live, I hope you will some day meet with consolation you had not expected. You were petitioning to see your friend Signor Maroncelli."

"So many times, that I no longer hope for it."

"Hope, hope, sir; and repeat your request."

I did so that very day. The superintendent also gave me hopes; and added, that probably I should not only be permitted to see him, but that he would attend on me, and most likely become my undivided companion.

It appeared, that as all the state prisoners had fallen ill, the governor had requested permission from Vienna to have them placed two and two, in order that one might assist the other in case of extreme need.

I had also solicited the favour of writing to my family for the last time.

Towards the end of the second week, my attack reached its crisis, and the danger was over. I had begun to sit up, when one morning my door opened, and the superintendent, Schiller, and the doctor, all apparently rejoicing, came into my apartment. The first ran towards me, exclaiming,

"We have got permission for Maroncelli to bear you company; and you may write to your parents."

Joy deprived me both of breath and speech, and the superintendent, who in his kindness had not been quite prudent, believed that he had killed me. On recovering my senses, and recollecting the good news, I entreated not to have it delayed. The physician consented, and my friend Maroncelli was conducted to my bedside. Oh! what a moment was that.

"Are you alive?" each of us exclaimed.

"Oh, my friend, my brother—what a happy day have we lived to see! God's name be ever blessed for it." But our joy was mingled with as deep compassion. Maroncelli was less surprised upon seeing me, reduced as I was, for he knew that I had been very ill, but though aware how HE must have suffered, I could not have imagined he would be so extremely changed. He was hardly to be recognised; his once noble and handsome features were wholly consumed, as it were, by grief, by continual hunger, and by the bad air of his dark, subterranean dungeon.

Nevertheless, to see, to hear, and to be near each other was a great comfort. How much had we to communicate—to recollect—and to talk over! What delight in our mutual compassion, what sympathy in all our ideas! Then we were equally agreed upon subjects of religion; to hate only ignorance and barbarism, but not man, not individuals, and on the other hand to commiserate the ignorant and the barbarous, and to pray for their improvement.

CHAPTER LXXV.

I WAS now presented with a sheet of paper and ink, in order that I might write to my parents.

As in point of strictness the permission was only given to a dying man, desirous of bidding a last adieu to his family,

I was apprehensive that the letter being now of a different tenour, it would no longer be sent upon its destination. I confined myself to the simple duty of beseeching my parents, my brothers, and my sisters, to resign themselves without a murmur to bear the lot appointed me, even as I myself was resigned to the will of God.

This letter was, nevertheless, forwarded, as I subsequently learnt. It was, in fact, the only one which, during so long protracted a captivity, was received by my family; the rest were all detained at Vienna. My companions in misfortune were equally cut off from all communication with their friends and families.

We repeatedly solicited that we might be allowed the use of pen and paper for purposes of study, and that we might purchase books with our own money. Neither of these petitions was granted.

The governor, meanwhile, permitted us to read our own books among each other. We were indebted also to his goodness for an improvement in our diet; but it did not continue. He had consented that we should be supplied from the kitchen of the superintendent instead of that of the contractor; and some fund had been put apart for that purpose. The order, however, was not confirmed; but in the brief interval it was in force my health had greatly improved. It was the same with Maroncelli; but for the unhappy Oroboni it came too late. He had received for his companion the advocate Solera, and afterwards the priest, Dr. Fortini.

We were no sooner distributed through the different prisons than the prohibition to appear or to converse at our windows was renewed, with threats that, if detected, the offenders would be consigned to utter solitude. We often, it is true, broke through this prison-law, and saluted each other from our windows, but no longer engaged in long conversations as we had before done.

In point of disposition, Maroncelli and I were admirably suited to each other. The courage of the one sustained the other; if one became violent the other soothed him; if buried in grief or gloom, he sought to rouse him; and one friendly smile was often enough to mitigate the severity of our sufferings, and reconcile each other to life.

So long as we had books, we found them a delightful relief, not only by reading, but by committing them to memory. We also examined, compared, criticised, and collated, &c. We read and we reflected great part of the day in silence, and reserved the feast of conversation for the hours of dinner, for our walks, and the evenings.

While in his subterranean abode, Maroncelli had composed a variety of poems of high merit. He recited them and produced others. Many of these I committed to memory. It is astonishing with what facility I was enabled, by this exercise, to repeat very extensive compositions, to give them additional polish, and bring them to the highest possible perfection of which they were susceptible, even had I written them down with the utmost care. Maroncelli did the same, and, by degrees, retained by heart many thousand lyric verses, and epics of different kinds. It was thus, too, I composed the tragedy of *Leoniero da Dertona*, and various other works.

CHAPTER LXXVI.

Count Oroboni, after lingering through a wretched winter and the ensuing spring, found himself much worse during the summer. He was seized with a spitting of blood, and a dropsy ensued. Imagine our affliction on learning that he was dying so near us, without a possibility of our rendering him the last sad offices, separated only as we were by a dungeon-wall.

Schiller brought us tidings of him. The unfortunate young Count, he said, was in the greatest agonies, yet he retained his admirable firmness of mind. He received the spiritual consolations of the chaplain, who was fortunately acquainted with the French language. He died on the 13th of June, 1823. A few hours before he expired, he spoke of his aged father, eighty years of age, was much affected, and shed tears. Then resuming his serenity, he said, "But why thus lament the destiny of the most fortunate of all those so dear to me; for *he* is on the eve of rejoining me in the realms of eternal peace?" The last words he uttered, were, "I forgive all my enemies; I do it from my heart!" His eyes were closed by his friend, Dr. Fortini, a most religious and amiable man, who had been intimate with him from his childhood. Poor Oroboni! how bitterly we felt his death when the first sad tidings reached us! Ah! we heard the voices and the steps of those who came to remove his body! We watched from our window the hearse, which, slow and solemnly, bore him to that cemetery within our view. It was drawn thither by two of the common convicts, and followed by four of the guards. We kept our eyes fixed upon the sorrowful spectacle, without speaking a word, till it entered the churchyard. It passed through, and stopped at last in a corner, near a new-made grave. The ceremony was brief; almost immediately the hearse, the convicts, and the guards were observed to return. One of the last was Kubitzky. He said to me, "I have marked the exact spot where he is buried, in order that some relation or friend may be enabled some day to remove his poor bones, and lay them in his own country. It was a noble thought, and surprised me in a man so wholly uneducated; but I could not speak. How often had the unhappy Count gazed from his window upon that dreary looking cemetery, as he observed, "I must try to get accustomed to the idea of being carried thither; yet I confess that such an idea makes me shiver. It is strange, but I cannot help thinking that we shall not rest so well in these foreign parts as in our own beloved land." He would then laugh, and exclaim, "What childishness is this! when a garment is worn out, and done with, does it signify where we throw it aside?" At other times, he would say, "I am continually preparing for death, but I should die more willingly upon one condition—just to enter my father's house once more, embrace his knees, hear his voice blessing me, and die!" He then sighed and added, "But if this cup, my God, cannot pass from me, may thy will be done." Upon the morning of his death he also said, as he pressed a crucifix, which Kral brought him, to his lips; "Thou, Lord, who wert Divine, hadst also a horror of death, and didst say, *If it be possible, let this cup pass from me*, oh, pardon if I too say it; but I will repeat also with Thee, *Nevertheless, not as I will, but as thou willest it!*"

CHAPTER LXXVII.

After the death of Oroboni, I was again taken ill. I expected very soon to rejoin him, and I ardently desired it. Still, I could not have parted with Maroncelli without regret. Often, while seated on his straw-bed, he read or recited poetry to withdraw my mind, as well as his own, from reflecting upon our misfortunes, I gazed on him, and thought with pain, When I am gone, when you see them bearing me hence, when you gaze at the cemetery, you will look more sorrowful than now. I would then offer a secret prayer that another companion might be given him, as capable of appreciating all his worth.

I shall not mention how many different attacks I suffered, and with how much difficulty I recovered from them. The assistance I received from my friend Maroncelli, was like that of an attached brother. When it became too great an effort for me to speak, he was silent; he saw the exact moment when his conversation would soothe or enliven me, he dwelt upon subjects most congenial to my feelings, and he continued or varied them as he judged most agreeable to me. Never did I meet with a nobler spirit; he had few equals, none, whom I knew, superior to him. Strictly just, tolerant, truly religious, with a remarkable confidence in human virtue, he added to these qualities an admirable taste for the beautiful, whether in art or nature, and a fertile imagination teeming with poetry; in short, all those engaging dispositions of mind and heart best calculated to endear him to me.

Still, I could not help grieving over the fate of Oroboni while, at the same time, I indulged the soothing reflection that he was freed from all his sufferings, that they were rewarded with a better world, and that in the midst of the enjoyments he had won, he must have that of beholding me with a friend no less attached to me than he had been himself. I felt a secret assurance that he was no longer in a place of expiation, though I ceased not to pray for him. I often saw him in my dreams, and he seemed to pray for me; I tried to think that they were not mere dreams; that they were manifestations of his blessed spirit, permitted by God for my consolation. I should not be believed were I to describe the excessive vividness of such dreams, if such they were, and the delicious serenity which they left in my mind for many days after. These, and the religious sentiments entertained by Maroncelli, with his tried friendship, greatly alleviated my afflictions. The sole idea which tormented me was the possibility of this excellent friend also being snatched from me; his health having been much broken, so as to threaten his dissolution ere my own sufferings drew to a close. Every time he was taken ill, I trembled; and when he felt better, it was a day of rejoicing for me. Strange, that there should be a fearful sort of pleasure, anxious yet intense, in these alternations of hope and dread, regarding the existence of the only object left you on earth. Our lot was one of the most painful; yet to esteem, to love each other as we did, was to us a little paradise, the one green spot in the desert of our lives; it was all we had left, and we bowed our heads in thankfulness to the Giver of all good, while awaiting the hour of his summons.

CHAPTER LXXVIII.

It was now my favourite wish that the chaplain who had attended me in my first illness, might be allowed to visit us as our confessor. But instead of complying with our request, the governor sent us an Augustine friar, called Father Battista, who was to confess us until an order came from Vienna, either to confirm the choice, or to nominate another in his place.

I was afraid we might suffer by the change, but was deceived. Father Battista was an excellent man, highly educated, of polished manners, and capable of reasoning admirably, even profoundly, upon the duties of man. We entreated him to visit us frequently; he came once a month, and oftener when in his power to do so; he always brought us some book or other with the governor's permission, and informed us from the abbot that the entire library of the convent was at our service. This was a great event for us; and we availed ourselves of the offer during several months.

After confession, he was accustomed to converse with us and gave evidence of an upright and elevated mind, capable of estimating the intrinsic dignity and sanctity of the human mind. We had the advantage of his enlightened views, of his affection, and his friendship for us during the space of a year. At first I confess that I distrusted him, and imagined that we should soon discover him putting out his feelers to induce us to make imprndent disclosures. In a prisoner of state this sort of diffidence is but too natural; but how great the satisfaction we experience when it disappears, and when we acknowledge in the interpreter of God no other zeal than that inspired by the cause of God and of humanity.

He had a most efficacious method of administering consolation. For instance, I accused myself of flying into a rage at the rigours imposed upon me by the prison discipline. He discoursed upon the virtue of suffering with resignation, and pardoning our enemies; and depicted in lively colours the miseries of life—in ranks and conditions opposite to my own. He had seen much of life, both in cities and the country, known men of all grades, and deeply reflected upon human oppression and injustice. He painted the operation of the passions, and the habits of various social classes. He described them to me throughout as the strong and the weak, the oppressors and the oppressed: and the necessity we were under, either of hating our fellow-man or loving him by a generous effort of compassion.

The examples he gave to show me the prevailing character of misfortune in the mass of human beings, and the good which was to be hence derived, had nothing singular in them; in fact they were obvious to view; but he recounted them in language so just and forcible, that I could not but admit the deductions he wished to draw from them.

The oftener he repeated his friendly reproaches, and his noble exhortations, the more was I incited to the love of virtue; I no longer felt capable of resentment—I could have laid down my life, with the permission of God, for the least of my fellow-creatures, and I yet blest His holy name for having created me—MAN!

Wretch that he is who remains ignorant of the sublime duty of confession! Still more wretched who, to shun the common herd, as he believes, feels himself called upon to regard it with scorn! Is it not a truth that even when we know what is required of us to be good, that self-knowledge is a dead letter to us? reading and reflection are insufficient to impel us to it; it is only the living speech of a man gifted with power which can here be of avail. The soul is shaken to its centre, the impressions it receives are more profound and lasting. In the brother who speaks to you, there is a life, and a living and breathing spirit—one which you can always consult, and which you will vainly seek for, either in books or in your own thoughts.

CHAPTER LXXIX.

In the beginning of 1824 the superintendent, who had his office at one end of our gallery, removed elsewhere, and the chambers, along with others, were converted into additional prisons. By this, alas, we were given to understand that other prisoners of state were expected from Italy.

They arrived in fact very shortly—a third special commission was at hand—and they were all in the circle of my friends or my acquaintance. What was my grief when I was told their names! Borsieri was one of my oldest friends. To Confalonieri I had been attached a less time indeed, but not the less ardently. Had it been in my power, by taking upon myself the *carcere durissimo*, or any other imaginable torment, how willingly would I have purchased their liberation. Not only would I have laid down my life for them,—for what is it to give one's life? I would have continued to suffer for them.

It was then I wished to obtain the consolations of Father Battista; but they would not permit him to come near me.

New orders to maintain the severest discipline were received from Vienna. The terrace on which we walked was hedged in by stockades, and in such a way that no one, even with the use of a telescope, could perceive our movements.

We could no longer catch the beautiful prospect of the surrounding hills, and part of the city of Brünn which lay below. Yet this was not enough. To reach the terrace, we were obliged, as before stated, to traverse the courtyard, and a number of persons could perceive us. That we might be concealed from every human eye, we were prohibited from crossing it, and we were confined in our walk to a small passage close to our gallery, with a north aspect similar to that of our dungeons.

To us such a change was a real misfortune, and it grieved us. There were innumerable little advantages and refreshments to our worn and wasted spirits in the walk of which we were deprived. The sight of the superintendent's children; their smiles and caresses; the scene where I had taken leave of their mother; the occasional chit-chat with the old smith, who had his forge there; the joyous songs of one of the captains accompanied by his guitar; and last not least, the innocent badinage of a young Hungarian fruiteress—the corporal's wife, who flirted with my companions—were among what we had lost. She had, in fact, taken a great fancy for Maroncelli.

Previous to his becoming my companion, he had made a little of her acquaintance; but was so sincere, so dignified, and so simple in his intentions as to be quite insensible of the impression he had produced. I informed him of it, and he would not believe I was serious, though he declared that he would take care to preserve a greater distance. Unluckily the more he was reserved, the more did the lady's fancy for him seemed to increase.

It so happened that her window was scarcely above a yard higher than the level of the terrace; and in an instant she was at our side with the apparent intention of putting out some linen to dry, or to perform some other household offices; but in fact to gaze at my friend, and, if possible, enter into conversation with him.

Our poor guards, half wearied to death for want of sleep, had, meantime, eagerly caught at an opportunity of throwing themselves on the grass, just in this corner, where they were no longer under the eye of their superiors. They fell asleep; and meanwhile Maroncelli was not a little perplexed what to do, such was the resolute affection borne him by the fair Hungarian. I was no less puzzled; for an affair of the kind, which, elsewhere, might have supplied matter for some merriment, was here very serious, and might lead to some very unpleasant result. The unhappy cause of all this had one of those countenances which tell you at once their character—the habit of being virtuous, and the necessity of being esteemed. She was not beautiful, but had a remarkable expression of elegance in her whole manner and deportment; her features, though not regular, fascinated when she smiled, and with every change of sentiment.

Were it my purpose to dwell upon love affairs, I should have no little to relate respecting this virtuous but unfortunate woman—now deceased. Enough that I have alluded to one of the few adventures which marked my prison-hours.

CHAPTER LXXX.

THE increasing rigour of our prison discipline rendered our lives one unvaried scene. The whole of 1824, of 1825, of 1826, of 1827, presented the same dull, dark aspect; and how we lived through years like these is wonderful. We were forbidden the use of books. The prison was one immense tomb, though without the peace and unconsciousness of death. The director of police came every month to institute the most strict and minute search, assisted by a lieutenant and guards. They made us strip to the skin, examined the seams of our garments, and ripped up the straw bundles called our beds in pursuit of—nothing. It was a secret affair, intended to take us by surprise, and had something about it which always irritated me exceedingly, and left me in a violent fever.

The preceding years had appeared to me very unhappy, yet I now remembered them with regret. The hours were fled when I could read my Bible, and Homer, from whom I had imbibed such a passionate admiration of his glorious language. Oh, how it irked me to be unable to prosecute my study of him! And there were Dante, Petrarch, Shakespeare, Byron, Walter Scott, Schiller, Goethe, &c.—how many friends, how many innocent and true delights were withheld from me. Among these I included a number of works, also, upon Christian knowledge; those of Bourdaloue, Pascal, "The Imitation of Christ," "The Filotea," &c., books usually read with narrow, illiberal views by those who exult in every little defect of taste, and at every common-place thought which impels the reader to throw them for ever aside; but which, when perused in a true spirit free from scandalous or malignant construction, discover a mine of deep philosophy, and vigorous nutriment both for the intellect and the heart. A few of certain religious books, indeed, were sent us, as a present, by the Emperor, but with an absolute prohibition to receive works of any other kind adapted for literary occupation.

This imperial gift of ascetic productions arrived in 1825 by a Dalmatian Confessor, Father Stefano Paulowich, afterwards Bishop of Cattaro, who was purposely sent from Vienna. We were indebted to him for performing mass, which had been before refused us, on the plea that they could not convey us into the church and keep us separated into two and two as the imperial law prescribed. To avoid such infraction we now went to mass in three groups; one being placed upon the tribune of the organ, another under the tribune, so as not to be visible, and the third in a small oratory, from which was a view into the church through a grating. On this occasion Maroncelli and I had for companions six convicts, who had received sentence before we came, but no two were allowed to speak to any other two in the group. Two of them, I found, had been my neighbours in the Piombi at Venice.

We were conducted by the guards to the post assigned us, and then brought back after mass in the same manner, each couple into their former dungeon. A Capuchin friar came to celebrate mass; the good man ended every rite with a "let us pray" for "liberation from chains," and "to set the prisoner free," in a voice which trembled with emotion.

On leaving the altar he cast a pitying look on each of the three groups, and bowed his head sorrowfully in secret prayer.

CHAPTER LXXXI.

In 1825 Schiller was pronounced past his service from infirmity and old age; though put in guard over some other prisoners, not thought to require equal vigilance and care. It was a trying thing to part from him, and he felt it as well as we. Kral, a man not inferior to him in good disposition, was at first his successor. But he too was removed, and we had a jailor of a very harsh and distant manner, wholly devoid of emotion, though not intrinsically bad.

I felt grieved; Schiller, Kral, and Kubitzky, but in particular the two former, had attended us in our extreme sufferings with the affection of a father or a brother. Though incapable of violating their trust, they knew how to do their duty without harshness of any kind. If there were something hard in the forms, they took the sting out of them as much as possible by various ingenious traits and turns of a benevolent mind. I was sometimes angry at them, but they took all I said in good part. They wished us to feel that they had become attached to us; and they rejoiced when we expressed as much, and approved of anything they did.

From the time Schiller left us, he was frequently ill; and we inquired after him with a sort of filial anxiety. When he sufficiently recovered, he was in the habit of coming to walk under our windows; we hailed him, and he would look up with a melancholy smile, at the same time addressing the sentinels in a voice we could overhear: "*Da sind meine Sohne!* there are my sons."

Poor old man! how sorry I was to see him almost staggering along, with the weight of increasing infirmities, so near us, and without being enabled to offer him even my arm.

Sometimes he would sit down upon the grass, and read. They were the same books he had often lent me. To please me, he would repeat the titles to the sentinels, or recite some extract from them, and then look up at me, and nod. After several attacks of apoplexy, he was conveyed to the military hospital, where in a brief period he died. He left some hundreds of florins, the fruit of long savings. These he had already lent, indeed, to such of his old military comrades as most required them; and when he found his end approaching, he called them all to his bedside, and said: "I have no relations left; I wish each of you to keep what I have lent you, for my sake. I only ask that you will pray for me."

One of these friends had a daughter of about eighteen, and who was Schiller's god-daughter. A few hours before his death, the good old man sent for her. He could not speak distinctly, but he took a silver ring from his finger, and placed it upon hers. He then kissed her, and shed tears over her. The poor girl sobbed as if her heart would break, for she was tenderly attached to him. He took a handkerchief, and, as if trying to soothe her, he dried her eyes. Lastly, he took hold of her hands, and placed them upon his eyes; and those eyes were closed for ever.

CHAPTER LXXXII.

All human consolations were one by one fast deserting us, and our sufferings still increased. I resigned myself to the will of God, but my spirit groaned. It seemed as if my mind, instead of becoming inured to evil, grew more keenly susceptible of pain. One day there was secretly brought to me a page of the Augsburgh Gazette, in which I found the strangest assertions respecting myself on occasion of mention being made of one of my sisters retiring into a nunnery. It stated as follows:—"The Signora Maria Angiola Pellico, daughter, &c., took the veil (on such a day) in the monastery of the Visitazione at Turin, &c. This lady is sister to the author of *Francesca da Rimini*, Silvio Pellico, who was recently liberated from the fortress of Spielberg, being pardoned by his Majesty, the emperor —a trait of clemency worthy of so magnanimous a sovereign, and a subject of gratulation to the whole of Italy, inasmuch as," &c., &c.

And here followed some eulogiums which I omit. I could not conceive for what reason the hoax relating to the gracious pardon had been invented. It seemed hardly probable it could be a mere freak of the editor's; and was it then intended as some stroke of oblique German policy? Who knows! However this may be, the names of Maria Angiola were precisely those of my younger sister, and doubtless they must have been copied from the Turin Gazette into other papers. Had that excellent girl, then, really become a nun? Had she taken this step in consequence of the loss of her parents? Poor Maria! she would not permit me alone to suffer the deprivations of a prison; she too would seclude herself from the world. May God grant her patience and self-denial, far beyond what I have evinced; for often I know will that angel, in her solitary cell, turn her thoughts and her prayers towards me. Alas, it may be, she will impose on herself some rigid penance, in the hope that God may alleviate the sufferings of her brother! These reflections agitated me greatly, and my heart bled. Most likely my own misfortunes had helped to shorten the days both of my father and my mother; for, were they living, it would be hardly possible that my Marietta would have deserted our parental roof. At length the idea oppressed me with the weight of absolute certainty, and I fell into a wretched and agonised state of mind. Maroncelli was no less affected than myself. The next day he composed a beautiful elegy upon "the sister of the prisoner." When he had completed it, he read it to me. How grateful was I for such a proof of his affection for me! Among the infinite number of poems which had been written upon similar subjects, not one, probably, had been composed in prison, for the brother of the nun, and by his companion in captivity and chains. What a field for pathetic and religious ideas was here, and Maroncelli filled his lyre with wild and pathetic tones, which drew delicious tears from my eyes.

It was thus friendship sweetened all my woes. Seldom from that day did I forget to turn my thoughts long and fondly to some sacred asylum of virgin hearts, and that one beloved form did not rise before my fancy, dressed in all that human piety and love can picture in a brother's heart. Often did I beseech Heaven to throw a charm round her religious solitude, and not permit that her imagination should paint in too horrible colours the sufferings of the sick and weary captive.

CHAPTER LXXXIII.

The reader must not suppose from the circumstance of my seeing the Gazette, that I was in the habit of hearing news, or could obtain any. No! though all the agents employed around me were kind, the system was such as to inspire the utmost terror. If there occurred the least clandestine proceeding, it was only when the danger was not felt—when not the least risk appeared. The extreme rareness of any such occurrences may be gathered from what has been stated respecting the ordinary and extraordinary searches which took place, morning, noon, and night, through every corner of our dungeons.

I had never a single opportunity of receiving any notice, however slight, regarding my family, even by secret means, beyond the allusions in the Gazette to my sister and myself. The fears I entertained lest my dear parents no longer survived were greatly augmented, soon after, by the manner in which the police director came to inform me that my relatives were well.

"His Majesty the Emperor," he said, "commands me to communicate to you good tidings of your relations at Turin."

I could not express my pleasure and my surprise at this unexpected circumstance; but I soon put a variety of questions to him as to their health: "Left you my parents, brothers, and sisters, at Turin? are they alive? if you have any letter from them pray let me have it."

"I can show you nothing. You must be satisfied. It is a mark of the Emperor's clemency to let you know even so much. The same favour is not shown to every one."

"I grant it is a proof of the Emperor's kindness; but you will allow it to be impossible for me to derive the least consolation from information like this. Which of my relations are well? have I lost no one?"

"I am sorry, sir, that I cannot state more than I have been directed." And he retired.

It must assuredly have been intended to console me by this indefinite allusion to my family. I felt persuaded that the Emperor had yielded to the earnest petition of some of my relatives to permit me to hear tidings of them, and that I was permitted to receive no letter in order to remain in the dark as to which of my dear family were now no more. I was the more confirmed in this supposition from the fact of receiving a similar communication a few months subsequently; but there was no letter, no further news.

It was soon perceived that so far from having been productive of satisfaction to me, such meagre tidings had thrown me into still deeper affliction, and I heard no more of my beloved family. The continual suspense, the distracting idea that my parents were dead, that my brothers also might be no more, that my sister Giuseppina was gone, and that Marietta was the sole survivor, and that in the agony of her sorrow she had thrown herself into a convent, there to close her unhappy days, still haunted my imagination, and completely alienated me from life.

Not unfrequently I had fresh attacks of the terrible disorders under which I had before suffered, with those of a still more painful kind, such as violent spasms of the stomach, exactly like *cholera morbus*, from the effects of which I hourly expected to die. Yes! and I fervently hoped and prayed that all might soon be over.

At the same time, nevertheless, whenever I cast a pitying glance at my no less weak and unfortunate companion—such is the strange contradiction of our nature—I felt my heart inly bleed at the idea of leaving him, a solitary prisoner, in such an abode; and again I wished to live.

CHAPTER LXXXIV.

THRICE, during my incarceration at Spielberg, there arrived persons of high rank to inspect the dungeons, and ascertain that there was no abuse of discipline. The first visitor was the Baron Von Münch, who, struck with compassion on seeing us so sadly deprived of light and air, declared that he would petition in our favour, to have a lantern placed over the outside of the pane in our dungeon doors, through which the sentinels could at any moment perceive us. His visit took place in 1825, and a year afterwards his humane suggestion was put in force. By this sepulchral light we could just catch a view of the walls, and prevent our knocking our heads in trying to walk. The second visit was that of the Baron Von Vogel. He found me in a lamentable state of health; and learning that the physician had declared that coffee would be very good for me, and that I could not obtain it, as being too great a luxury, he interested himself for me, and my old, delightful beverage, was ordered to be brought me. The third visit was from a lord of the court, with whose name I am not acquainted, between fifty and sixty years of age, and who, by his manners as well as his words, testified the sincerest compassion for us; at the same time lamenting that he could do nothing for us. Still, the expression of his sympathy—for he was really affected—was something, and we were grateful for it.

How strange, how irresistible, is the desire of the solitary prisoner to behold some one of his own species! It amounts almost to a sort of instinct, as if in order to avoid insanity, and its usual consequence, the tendency to self-destruction. The Christian religion, so abounding in views of humanity, forgets not to enumerate amongst its works of mercy the visiting of the prisoner. The mere aspect of man, his look of commiseration, and his willingness, as it were, to share with you, and bear a part of your heavy burden, even when you know he cannot relieve you, has something that sweetens your bitter cup.

Perfect solitude is doubtless of advantage to some minds; but far more so if not carried to an extreme, and relieved by some little intercourse with society. Such at least is my constitution. If I do not behold my fellow-men, my affections become restricted to too confined a circle, and I begin to dislike all others; while, if I continue in communication with an ordinary number, I learn to regard the whole of mankind with affection.

Innumerable times, I am sorry to confess, I have been so exclusively occupied with a few, and so averse to the many, as to be almost terrified at the feelings I experienced. I would then approach the window, desirous of catching some new features, and thought myself happy when the sentinel passed not too closely to the wall, if I got a single glance of him, or if he lifted up his head upon hearing me cough—more especially if he had a good-natured countenance; when he showed the least feeling of pity, I felt a singular emotion of pleasure, as if that unknown soldier had been one of my intimate friends.

If, the next time, he passed by in a manner that prevented my seeing him, or took no notice of me, I felt as much mortified as some poor lover, when he finds that the beloved object wholly neglects him.

CHAPTER LXXXV.

In the adjoining prison, once occupied by Oroboni, D. Marco Fortini and Antonio Villa were now confined. The latter, once as strong as Hercules, was nearly famished the first year, and when a better allowance was granted he had wholly lost the power of digestion. He lingered a long time, and when reduced almost to the last extremity, he was removed into a somewhat more airy prison. The pestilential atmosphere of these narrow receptacles, so much resembling real tombs, was doubtless very injurious to others as well as to him. But the remedy sought for was too late or insufficient to remove the cause of his sufferings. He had scarcely been a month in this spacious prison, when, in consequence of bursting several blood-vessels, and his previously broken health, he died.

He was attended by his fellow-prisoner, D. Fortini, and by the Abate Paulowich, who hastened from Vienna upon hearing that he was dying. Although I had not been on the same intimate terms with him as with Count Oroboni, his death a good deal affected me. He had parents and a wife, all most tenderly attached to him. *He*, indeed, was more to be envied than regretted; but, alas, for the unhappy survivors to whom he was everything! He had, moreover, been my neighbour when under the *Piombi*. Tremerello had brought me several of his poetical pieces, and had conveyed to him some lines from me in return. There was sometimes a depth of sentiment and pathos in his poems which interested me. I seemed to become still more attached to him after he was gone; learning, as I did from the guards, how dreadfully he had suffered. It was with difficulty, though truly religious, that he could resign himself to die. He experienced to the utmost the horror of that final step, while he blessed the name of the Lord, and called upon His name with tears streaming from his eyes. "Alas," he said, "I cannot conform my will unto thine, yet how willingly would I do it; do thou work this happy change in me!" He did not possess the same courage as Oroboni, but followed his example in forgiving all his enemies.

At the close of the year (1826) we one evening heard a suppressed noise in the gallery, as if persons were stealing along. Our hearing had become amazingly acute in distinguishing different kinds of noises. A door was opened; and we knew it to be that of the advocate Solera. Another! it was that of Fortini! There followed a whispering, but we could tell the voice of the police director, suppressed as it was. What could it be? a search at so late an hour! and for what reason?

In a brief space, we heard steps again in the gallery; and ah! more plainly we recognised the voice of our excellent Fortini: "Unfortunate as I am! excuse it? go out! I have forgotten a volume of my breviary!" And we then heard him run back to fetch the book mentioned, and rejoin the police. The door of the staircase opened, and we heard them go down. In the midst of our alarm we learnt that our two good friends had just received a pardon; and although we regretted we could not follow them, we rejoiced in their unexpected good fortune.

CHAPTER LXXXVI.

The liberation of our two companions brought no alteration in the discipline observed towards us. Why, we asked ourselves, were they set at liberty, condemned as they had been, like us, the one to twenty, the other to fifteen years' imprisonment, while no sort of favour was shown to the rest?

Were the suspicions against those who were still consigned to captivity more strong, or did the disposition to pardon the whole, at brief intervals of time, and two together, really exist? We continued in suspense for some time. Upwards of three months elapsed, and we heard of no fresh instances of pardon. Towards the end of 1827, we considered that December might be fixed on as the anniversary of some new liberations; but the month expired, and nothing of the kind occurred.

Still we indulged the expectation until the summer of 1828, when I had gone through seven years and a half of my punishment—equivalent, according to the Emperor's declaration, to the fifteen, if the infliction of it were to be dated from the term of my arrest. If, on the other hand, it were to be calculated, not from the period of my trial, as was most probable, but from that of the publication of my sentence, the seven years and a half would only be completed in 1829.

Yet all these periods passed over, and there was no appearance of a remittance of punishment. Meantime, even before the liberation of Solera and Fortini, Maroncelli was ill with a bad tumour upon his knee. At first the pain was not great, and he only limped as he walked. It then grew very irksome to him to bear his irons, and he rarely went out to walk. One autumnal morning he was desirous of breathing the fresh air; there was a fall of snow, and unfortunately in walking his leg failed him, and he came to the ground. This accident was followed by acute pain in his knee. He was carried to his bed; for he was no longer able to remain in an upright position. When the physician came, he ordered his irons to be taken off; but the swelling increased to an enormous size, and became more painful every day. Such at length were the sufferings of my unhappy friend, that he could obtain no rest either in bed or out of it. When compelled to move about, to rise or to lie down, it was necessary to take hold of the bad leg and carry it as he went with the utmost care; and the most trifling motion brought on the most severe pangs. Leaches, baths, caustics, and fomentations of different kinds, were all found ineffectual, and seemed only to aggravate his torments. After the use of caustics, suppuration followed; the tumour broke out into wounds, but even these failed to bring relief to the suffering patient.

Maroncelli was thus far more unfortunate than myself; although my sympathy for him caused me real pain and suffering, I was glad, however, to be near him, to attend to all his wants, and to perform all the duties of a brother and a friend. It soon became evident that his leg would never heal: he considered his death as near at hand, and yet he lost nothing of his admirable calmness or his courage. The sight of his sufferings at last was almost more than I could bear

CHAPTER LXXXVII.

STILL, in this deplorable condition, he continued to compose verses, he sang, and he conversed; and all this he did to encourage me, by disguising from me a part of what he suffered. He lost his powers of digestion, he could not sleep, was reduced to a skeleton, and very frequently swooned away. Yet the moment he was restored he rallied his spirits, and, smiling, bade me be not afraid. It is indescribable what he suffered during many months. At length a consultation was to be held; the head physician was called in, approved of all his colleague had done, and, without expressing a decisive opinion, took his leave. A few minutes after, the superintendent entered, and addressing Maroncelli,

"The head physician did not venture to express his real opinion in your presence; he feared you would not have fortitude to bear so terrible an announcement. I have assured him, however, that you are possessed of courage."

"I hope," replied Maroncelli, "that I have given some proof of it in bearing this dreadful torture without howling out. Is there anything he would propose?"

"Yes, sir, the amputation of the limb: only perceiving how much your constitution is broken down, he hesitates to advise you. Weak as you are, could you support the operation? will you run the risk——"

"Of dying? and shall I not equally die if I go on, without ending this diabolical torture?"

"We will send off an account, then, direct to Vienna, soliciting permission, and the moment it comes you shall have your leg cut off."

"What! does it require a *permit* for this?"

"Assuredly, sir," was the reply.

In about a week a courier arrived from Vienna with the expected news.

My sick friend was carried from his dungeon into a larger room, for permission to have his leg cut off had just arrived. He begged me to follow him: "I may die under the knife, and I should wish, in that case, to expire in your arms." I promised, and was permitted to accompany him. The sacrament was first administered to the unhappy prisoner, and we then quietly awaited the arrival of the surgeons. Maroncelli filled up the interval by singing a hymn. At length they came; one was an able surgeon, to superintend the operation, from Vienna; but it was the privilege of our ordinary prison apothecary, and he would not yield to the man of science, who must be contented to look on. The patient was placed on the side of a couch, with his leg down, while I supported him in my arms. It was to be cut above the knee; first, an incision was made, the depth of an inch—then through the muscles—and the blood flowed in torrents: the arteries were next taken up with ligatures, one by one. Next came the saw. This lasted some time, but Maroncelli never uttered a cry. When he saw them carrying his leg away, he cast on it one melancholy look, then turning towards the surgeon, he said, "You have freed me from an enemy, and I have no money to give you." He saw a rose, in a glass, placed in a window: "May I beg of you to bring me hither that flower?" I brought it to him; and he then offered it to the surgeon with an indescribable air of good-nature: "See, I have nothing else to give you in token of my gratitude." He took it as it was meant, and even wiped away a tear.

CHAPTER LXXXVIII.

THE surgeons had supposed that the hospital of Spielberg would provide all that was requisite except the instruments, which they brought with them. But after the amputation, it was found that a number of things were wanting; such as linen, ice, bandages, &c. My poor friend was thus compelled to wait two hours before these articles were brought from the city. At length he was laid upon his bed, and the ice applied to the trunk of the bleeding thigh. Next day it was dressed; but the patient was allowed to take no nourishment beyond a little broth, with an egg. When the risk of fever was over, he was permitted the use of restoratives; and an order from the Emperor directed that he should be supplied from the table of the superintendent till he was better.

The cure was completed in about forty days, after which we were conducted into our dungeon. This had been enlarged for us; that is, an opening was made in the wall so as to unite our old den to that once occupied by Oroboni, and subsequently by Villa. I placed my bed exactly in the same spot where Oroboni had died, and derived a mournful pleasure from thus approaching my friend, as it were, as nearly as possible. It appeared as if his spirit still hovered round me, and consoled me with manifestations of more than earthly love.

The horrible sight of Maroncelli's sufferings, both before and subsequently to the amputation of his leg, had done much to strengthen my mind. During the whole period, my health had enabled me to attend upon him, and I was grateful to God; but from the moment my friend assumed his crutches, and could supply his own wants, I began daily to decline. I suffered extremely from glandular swellings, and those were followed by pains of the chest, more oppressive than I had before experienced, attended with dizziness and spasmodic dysentery. "It is my turn now," thought I; "shall I show less patience than my companion?"

Every condition of life has its duties; and those of the sick consist of patience, courage, and continual efforts to appear not unamiable to the persons who surround them. Maroncelli, on his crutches, no longer possessed the same activity, and was fearful of not doing everything for me of which I stood in need. It was in fact the case, but I did all to prevent his being made sensible of it. Even when he had recovered his strength he laboured under many inconveniences. He complained, like most others after a similar operation, of acute pains in the nerves, and imagined that the part removed was still with him. Sometimes it was the toe, sometimes the leg, and at others the knee of the amputated limb which caused him to cry out. The bone, moreover, had been badly sawed, and pushed through the newly-formed flesh, producing frequent wounds. It required more than a year to bring the stump to a good state, when at length it hardened and broke out no more.

CHAPTER LXXXIX.

New evils, however, soon assailed my unhappy friend. One of the arteries, beginning at the joints of the hand, began to pain him, extending to other parts of his body; and then turned into a scorbutic sore. His whole person became covered with livid spots, presenting a frightful spectacle. I tried to reconcile myself to it, by considering that since it appeared we were to die here, it was better that one of us should be seized with the scurvy; it is a contagious disease, and must carry us off either together, or at a short interval from each other. We both prepared ourselves for death, and were perfectly tranquil. Nine years' imprisonment, and the grievous sufferings we had undergone, had at length familiarised us to the idea of the dissolution of two bodies so totally broken and in need of peace. It was time the scene should close, and we confided in the goodness of God, that we should be reunited in a place where the passions of men should cease, and where, we prayed, in spirit and in truth, that those who DID NOT LOVE US might meet us in peace, in a kingdom where only one Master, the supreme King of kings, reigned for evermore.

This malignant distemper had destroyed numbers of prisoners during the preceding years. The governor, upon learning that Maroncelli had been attacked by it, agreed with the physician, that the sole hope of remedy was in the fresh air. They were afraid of its spreading; and Maroncelli was ordered to be as little as possible within his dungeon. Being his companion, and also unwell, I was permitted the same privilege. We were permitted to be in the open air the whole time the other prisoners were absent from the walk, during two hours early in the morning, during the dinner, if we preferred it, and three hours in the evening, even after sunset.

There was one other unhappy patient, about seventy years of age, and in extremely bad health, who was permitted to bear us company. His name was Constantino Munari; he was of an amiable disposition, greatly attached to literature and philosophy, and agreeable in conversation.

Calculating my imprisonment, not from my arrest, but from the period of receiving my sentence, I had been seven years and a half (in the year 1829), according to the imperial decree, in different dungeons; and about nine from the day of my arrest. But this term, like the other, passed over, and there was no sign of remitting my punishment.

Up to the half of the whole term, my friend Maroncelli, Munari, and I had indulged the idea of a possibility of seeing once more our native land and our relations; and we frequently conversed with the warmest hopes and feelings upon the subject. August, September, and the whole of that year elapsed, and then we began to despair; nothing remained to relieve our destiny but our unaltered attachment for each other, and the support of religion, to enable us to close our latter prison hours with becoming dignity and resignation. It was then we felt the full value of friendship and religion, which threw a charm even over the darkness of our lot. Human hopes and promises had failed us; but God never forsakes the mourners and the captives who truly love and fear Him.

CHAPTER XC.

AFTER the death of Villa, the Abate Wrba was appointed our confessor, on occasion of the Abate Paulowich receiving a bishopric. He was a Moravian, professor of the gospel at Brünn, and an able pupil of the Sublime .Institute of Vienna. This was founded by the celebrated Frinl, then chaplain to the court. The members of the congregation are all priests, who, though already masters of theology, prosecute their studies under the Institution with the severest discipline. The views of the founder were admirable, being directed to the continual and general dissemination of true and profound science, among the Catholic clergy of Germany. His plans were for the most part successful, and are yet in extensive operation.

Being resident at Brünn, Wrba could devote more of his time to our society than Paulowich. He was a second father Battista, with the exception that he was not permitted to lend us any books. We held long discussions, from which I reaped great advantage, and real consolation. He was taken ill in 1829, and being subsequently called to other duties, he was unable to visit us more. We were much hurt, but we obtained as his successor the Abate Ziak, another learned and worthy divine. Indeed, among the whole German ecclesiastics we met with, not one showed the least disposition to pry into our political sentiments; not one but was worthy of the holy task he had undertaken, and imbued at once with the most edifying faith and enlarged wisdom.

They were all highly respectable, and inspired us with respect for the general Catholic clergy.

The Abate Ziak, both by precept and example, taught me to support my sufferings with calmness and resignation. He was afflicted with continual defluxions in his teeth, his throat, and his ears, and was, nevertheless, always calm and cheerful.

Maroncelli derived great benefit from exercise and open air; the eruptions, by degrees, disappeared; and both Munari and myself experienced equal advantage.

CHAPTER XCI.

It was the first of August, 1830. Ten years had elapsed since I was deprived of my liberty: for eight years and a half I had been subjected to hard imprisonment. It was Sunday, and, as on other holidays, we went to our accustomed station, whence we had a view from the wall of the valley and the cemetery below, where Oroboni and Villa now reposed. We conversed upon the subject, and the probability of our soon sharing their untroubled sleep. We had seated ourselves upon our accustomed bench, and watched the unhappy prisoners as they came forth and passed to hear mass, which was performed before our own. They were women, and were conducted into the same little chapel to which we resorted at the second mass.

It is customary with the Germans to sing hymns aloud during the celebration of mass. As the Austrian empire is composed partly of Germans and partly of Sclavonians, and the greater part of the prisoners at Spielberg consist of one or other of these people, the hymns are alternately sung in the German and the Sclavonian languages. Every festival, two sermons are preached, and the same division observed. It was truly delightful to us to hear the singing of the hymns, and the music of the organ which accompanied it. The voices of some of these women touched us to the heart. Unhappy ones! some of them were very young; whom love, or jealousy, or bad example, had betrayed into crime. I often think I can still hear their fervidly devotional hymn of the sanctus—*Heilig! heilig! heilig!*—Holy of holies; and the tears would start into my eyes. At ten o'clock the women used to withdraw, and we entered to hear mass. There I saw those of my companions in misfortune, who listened to the service from the tribune of the organ, and from whom we were separated only by a single grate, whose pale features and emaciated bodies, scarcely capable of dragging their irons, bore witness to their woes.

After mass we were conveyed back to our dungeons. About a quarter of an hour afterwards we partook of dinner. We were preparing our table, which consisted in putting a thin board upon a wooden target, and taking up our wooden spoons, when Signor Wagrath, the superintendent, entered our prison. "I am sorry to disturb you at dinner; but have the goodness to follow me; the Director of Police is waiting for us." As he was accustomed to come near us only for purposes of examination and search, we accompanied the superintendent to the audience room in no very good humour. There we found the Director of Police and the superintendent, the first of whom moved to us with rather more politeness than usual. He took out a letter, and stated in a hesitating, slow tone of voice, as if afraid of surprising us too greatly: "Gentlemen, ... I have . . . . the pleasure . . . . the honour, I mean. . . . . of . . of acquainting you that his Majesty the Emperor has granted you a further favour." Still he hesitated to inform us what this favour was; and we conjectured it must be some slight alleviation, some exemption from irksome labour,—to have a book, or, perhaps, less disagreeable diet. "Don't you understand?" he inquired. "No, sir!" was our reply; "have the goodness, if permitted, to explain yourself more fully."

"Then hear it! it is liberty for your two selves, and a third, who will shortly bear you company."

One would imagine that such an announcement would have thrown us into ecstasies of joy. We were so soon to see our parents, of whom we had not heard for so long a period; but the doubt that they were no longer in existence, was sufficient not only to moderate—it did not permit us to hail, the joys of liberty as we should have done.

"Are you dumb?" asked the director; "I thought to see you exulting at the news."

"May I beg you," replied I, "to make known to the Emperor our sentiments of gratitude; but if we are not favoured with some account of our families, it is impossible not to indulge in the greatest fear and anxiety. It is this consciousness which destroys the zest of all our joy."

He then gave Maroncelli a letter from his brother, which greatly consoled him. But he told me there was no account of my family, which made me the more fear that some calamity had befallen them.

"Now, retire to your apartments, and I will send you a third companion, who has received pardon."

We went, and awaited his arrival anxiously; wishing that all had alike been admitted to the same act of grace, instead of that single one. Was it poor old Munari? was it such, or such a one? Thus we went on guessing at every one we knew; when suddenly the door opened, and Signor Andrea Torrelli, of Brescia, made his appearance. We embraced him; and we could eat no more dinner that day. We conversed till towards evening, chiefly regretting the lot of the unhappy friends whom we were leaving behind us.

After sunset, the Director of Police returned to escort us from our wretched prison house. Our hearts, however, bled within us, as we were passing by the dungeons of so many of our countrymen whom we loved, and yet, alas, not to have them to share our liberty! Heaven knows how long they would be left to linger here! to become the gradual, but certain, prey of death.

We were each of us enveloped in a military great-coat, with a cap; and then, dressed as we were in our jail costume, but freed from our chains, we descended the funereal mount, and were conducted through the city into the police prisons.

It was a beautiful moonlight night. The roads, the houses, the people whom we met—every object appeared so strange, and yet so delightful, after the many years during which I had been debarred from beholding any similar spectacle!

CHAPTER XCII.

We remained at the police prisons, awaiting the arrival of the imperial commissioner from Vienna, who was to accompany us to the confines of Italy. Meantime, we were engaged in providing ourselves with linen and trunks, our own having all been sold, and defraying our prison expenses.

Five days afterwards, the commissary was announced, and the director consigned us over to him, delivering, at the same time, the money which we had brought with us to Spielberg, and the amount derived from the sale of our trunks and books, both which were restored to us on reaching our destination.

The expense of our journey was defrayed by the Emperor, and in a liberal manner. The commissary was Herr Von Noe, a gentleman employed in the office of the minister of police. The charge could not have been intrusted to a person every way more competent, as well from education as from habit; and he treated us with the greatest respect.

I left Brünn, labouring under extreme difficulty of breathing; and the motion of the carriage increased it to such a degree, that it was expected I should hardly survive during the evening. I was in a high fever the whole of the night; and the commissary was doubtful whether I should be able to continue my journey even as far as Vienna. I begged to go on; and we did so, but my sufferings were excessive. I could neither eat, drink, nor sleep.

I reached Vienna more dead than alive. We were well accommodated at the general directory of police. I was placed in bed, a physician called in, and after being bled, I found myself sensibly relieved. By means of strict diet, and the use of digitalis, I recovered in about eight days. My physician's name was Singer; and he devoted the most friendly attentions to me.

I had become extremely anxious to set out; the more so from an account of the *three days* having arrived from Paris. The Emperor had fixed the day of our liberation exactly on that when the revolution burst forth; and surely he would not now revoke it. Yet the thing was not improbable; a critical period appeared to be at hand, popular commotions were apprehended in Italy, and though we could not imagine we should be remanded to Spielberg, should we be permitted to return to our native country?

I affected to be stronger than I really was, and entreated we might be allowed to resume our journey. It was my wish, meantime, to be presented to his Excellency the Count Pralormo, envoy from Turin to the Austrian Court, to whom I was aware how much I had been indebted. He had left no means untried to procure my liberation; but the rule that we were to hold no communication with any one admitted of no exception. When sufficiently convalescent, a carriage was politely ordered for me, in which I might take an airing in the city; but accompanied by the commissary, and no other company. We went to see the noble church of St. Stephen, the delightful walks in the environs, the neighbouring Villa Lichtenstein, and lastly the imperial residence of Schoenbrunn.

While proceeding through the magnificent walks in the gardens, the Emperor approached, and the commissary hastily made us retire, lest the sight of our emaciated persons should give him pain.

CHAPTER XCIII.

We at length took our departure from Vienna, and I was enabled to reach Bruck. There my asthma returned with redoubled violence. A physician was called—Herr Jüdmann, a man of pleasing manners. He bled me, ordered me to keep my bed, and to continue the digitalis. At the end of two days I renewed my solicitations to continue our journey.

We proceeded through Austria and Stiria, and entered Carinthia without any accident; but on our arrival at the village of Feldkirchen, a little way from Klagenfurt, we were overtaken by a counter order from Vienna. We were to stop till we received farther directions. I leave the reader to imagine what our feelings must have been on this occasion. I had, moreover, the pain to reflect, that it would be owing to my illness if my two friends should now be prevented from reaching their native land. We remained five days at Feldkirchen, where the commissary did all in his power to keep up our spirits. He took us to the theatre to see a comedy, and permitted us one day to enjoy the chase. Our host and several young men of the country, along with the proprietor of a fine forest, were the hunters, and we were brought into a station favourable for commanding a view of the sports.

At length there arrived a courier from Vienna, with a fresh order for the commissary to resume his journey with us to the place first appointed. We congratulated each other, but my anxiety was still great, as I approached the hour when my hopes or fears respecting my family would be verified. How many of my relatives and friends might have disappeared during my ten years' absence!

The entrance into Italy on that side is not pleasing to the eye; you descend from the noble mountains of Germany into the Italian plains, through a long and sterile district, insomuch that travellers who have formed a magnificent idea of our country, begin to laugh, and imagine they have been purposely deluded with previous accounts of *La Bella Italia.*

The dismal view of that rude district served to make me more sorrowful. To see my native sky, to meet human features no more belonging to the north, to hear my native tongue from every lip affected me exceedingly; and I felt more inclined to tears than to exultation. I threw myself back in the carriage, pretending to sleep; but covered my face and wept. That night I scarcely closed my eyes: my fever was high, my whole soul seemed absorbed in offering up vows for my sweet Italy, and grateful prayers to Providence for having restored to her her captive son. Then I thought of my speedy separation from a companion with whom I had so long suffered, and who had given me so many proofs of more than fraternal affection, and I tortured my imagination with the idea of a thousand disasters which might have befallen my family. Not even so many years of captivity had deadened the energy and susceptibility of my feelings! but it was a susceptibility only to pain and sorrow.

I felt, too, on my return, a strange desire to visit Udine, and the lodging-house, where our two generous friends had assumed the character of waiters, and secretly stretched out to us the hand of friendship. But we passed that town to our left, and passed on our way.

CHAPTER XCIV.

PORDENONE, Conegliano, Ospedaletto, Vicenza, Verona, and Mantua, were all places which interested my feelings. In the first resided one of my friends, an excellent young man, who had survived the campaigns of Russia; Conegliano was the district whither, I was told by the under-jailors, poor Angiola had been conducted; and in Ospedaletto there had married and resided a young lady, who had more of the angel than the woman, and who, though now no more, I had every reason to remember with the highest respect. The whole of these places, in short, revived recollections more or less dear; and Mantua more than any other city. It appeared only yesterday that I had come with Lodovico in 1815, and paid another visit with Count Porro in 1820. The same roads, the same squares, the same palaces, and yet such a change in all social relations! So many of my connections snatched away for ever—so many exiled—one generation, I had beheld when infants, started up into manhood. Yet how painful not to be allowed to call at a single house, or to accost a single person we met.

To complete my misery, Mantua was the point of separation between Maroncelli and myself. We passed the night there, both filled with forebodings and regret. I felt agitated like a man on the eve of receiving his sentence.

The next morning I rose, and washed my face, in order to conceal from my friend how much I had given way to grief during the preceding night. I looked at myself in the glass, and tried to assume a quiet and even cheerful air. I then bent down in prayer, though ill able to command my thoughts; and hearing Maroncelli already upon his crutches, and speaking to the servant, I hastened to embrace him. We had both prepared ourselves, with previous exertions, for this closing interview, and we spoke to each other firmly, as well as affectionately. The officer appointed to conduct us to the borders of Romagna appeared; it was time to set out; we hardly knew how to speak another word; we grasped each other's hands again and again,—we parted; he mounted into his vehicle, and I felt as if I had been annihilated at a blow. I returned into my chamber, threw myself upon my knees, and prayed for my poor mutilated friend, thus separated from me, with sighs and tears.

I had known several celebrated men, but not one more affectionately sociable than Maroncelli; not one better educated in all respects, more free from sudden passion or ill-humour, more deeply sensible that virtue consists in continued exercises of tolerance, of generosity, and good sense. Heaven bless you, my dear companion in so many afflictions, and send you new friends who may equal me in my affection for you, and surpass me in true goodness.

CHAPTER XCV.

I SET out the same evening for Brescia. There I took leave of my other fellow-prisoner, Andrea Torrelli. The unhappy man had just heard that he had lost his mother, and the bitterness of his grief wrung my heart; yet, agonised as were my feelings from so many different causes, I could not help laughing at the following incident.

Upon the table of our lodging-house I found the following theatrical announcement:—*Francesca da Rimini; Opera da Musica*, &c. "Whose work is this?" I inquired of the waiter.

"Who versified it, and composed the music, I cannot tell, but it is the *Francesca da Rimini* which everybody knows."

"Everybody! you must be wrong there. I come from Germany, yet what do I know of your Francescas?" The waiter was a young man with rather a satirical cast of face, quite *Brescian;* and he looked at me with a contemptuous sort of pity. "What should you know, indeed, of our Francescas? why, no, sir, it is only *one* we speak of —*Francesca da Rimini*, to be sure, sir; I mean the tragedy of Signor Silvio Pellico. They have here turned it into an opera, spoiling it a little, no doubt, but still it is always Pellico."

"Ah, Silvio Pellico! I think I have heard his name. Is it not that same evil-minded conspirator who was condemned to death, and his sentence was changed to hard imprisonment, some eight or ten years ago?"

I should never have hazarded such a jest. He looked round him, fixed his eyes on me, showed a fine set of teeth, with no amiable intention; and I believe he would have knocked me down, had he not heard a noise close by us.

He went away muttering: "Ill-minded conspirator, indeed!" But before I left, he had found me out. He was half out of his wits; he could neither question, nor answer, nor write, nor walk, nor wait. He had his eyes continually upon me, he rubbed his hands, and addressing himself to every one near him; "*Sior si, Sior si;* Yes, sir! Yes, sir!" he kept stammering out, "coming! coming!"

Two days afterwards, on the 9th of September, I arrived with the commissary at Milan. On approaching the city, on seeing the cupola of the cathedral, in repassing the walk by Loretto, so well known, and so dear, on recognising the corso, the buildings, churches, and public places of every kind, what were my mingled feelings of pleasure and regret! I felt an intense desire to stop, and embrace once more my beloved friends. I reflected with bitter grief on those, whom, instead of meeting here, I had left in the horrible abode of Spielberg,—on those who were wandering in strange lands,—on those who were no more. I thought, too, with gratitude upon the affection shown me by the people; their indignation against all those who had calumniated me, while they had uniformly been the objects of my benevolence and esteem.

We went to take up our quarters at the *Bella Venezia.* It was here I had so often been present at our social meetings; here I had called upon so many distinguished foreigners; here a respectable, elderly *Signora* invited me in vain to follow her into Tuscany, foreseeing, she said, the misfortunes that would befall me if I remained at Milan. What affecting recollections! How rapidly past times came thronging over my memory, fraught with joy and grief!

The waiters at the hotel soon discovered who I was. The report spread, and towards evening a number of persons stopped in the square, and looked up at the windows. One, whose name I did not know, appeared to recognise me, and raising both his arms, made a sign of embracing me, as a welcome back to Italy.

And where were the sons of Porro; I may say my own sons? Why did I not see them there?

CHAPTER XCVI.

The commissary conducted me to the police, in order to present me to the director. What were my sensations upon recognising the house! it was my first prison. It was then I thought with pain of Melchiorre Gioja, on the rapid steps with which I had seen him pacing within those narrow walls, or sitting at his little table, recording his noble thoughts, or making signals to me; and his last look of sorrow, when forbidden longer to communicate with me. I pictured to myself his solitary grave, unknown to all who had so ardently loved him, and, while invoking peace to his gentle spirit, I wept.

Here, too, I called to mind the little dumb boy, the pathetic tones of Maddalene, my strange emotions of compassion for her, my neighbours the robbers, the assumed Louis XVII., and the poor prisoner who had carried the fatal letter, and whose cries under the infliction of the bastinado, had reached me.

These and other recollections appeared with all the vividness of some horrible dream; but most of all, I felt those two visits which my father had made me ten years before, when I last saw him. How the good old man had deceived himself in the expectation that I should so soon rejoin him at Turin! Could he then have borne the idea of a son's ten years' captivity, and in such a prison? But when these flattering hopes vanished, did he, and did my mother bear up against so unexpected a calamity? was I ever to see them again in this world? Had one, or which of them, died during the cruel interval that ensued?

Such was the suspense, the distracting doubt which yet clung to me. I was about to knock at the door of my home without knowing if they were in existence, or what other members of my beloved family were left me.

The director of police received me in a friendly manner. He permitted me to stay at the *Bella Venezia* with the imperial commissary, though I was not permitted to communicate with any one, and for this reason I determined to resume my journey the following morning. I obtained an interview, however, with the Piedmontese consul, to learn if possible some account of my relatives. I should have waited on him, but being attacked with fever, and compelled to keep my bed, I sent to beg the favour of his visiting me. He had the kindness to come immediately, and I felt truly grateful to him.

He gave me a favourable account of my father, and of my eldest brother. Respecting my mother, however, my other brother, and my two sisters, I could learn nothing.

Thus in part comforted, I could have wished to prolong the conversation with the consul, and he would willingly have gratified me had not his duties called him away. After he left me, I was extremely affected, but, as had so often happened, no tears came to give me relief. The habit of long, internal grief, seemed yet to prey upon my heart; to weep would have alleviated the fever which consumed me, and distracted my head with pain.

I called to Stündberger for something to drink. That good man was a sergeant of police at Vienna, though now filling the office of *valet-de-chambre* to the commissary.

But though not old, I perceived that his hand trembled in giving me the drink. This circumstance reminded me of Schiller, my beloved Schiller, when, on the day of my arrival at Spielberg, I ordered him, in an imperious tone, to hand me the jug of water, and he obeyed me.

How strange it was! The recollection of this, added to other feelings of the kind, struck, as it were, the rock of my heart, and tears began to flow.

CHAPTER XCVII.

The morning of the 10th of September, I took leave of the excellent commissary, and set out. We had only been acquainted with each other for about a month, and yet he was as friendly as if he had known me for years. His noble and upright mind was above all artifice, or desire of penetrating the opinions of others, not from any want of intelligence, but a love of that dignified simplicity which animates all honest men.

It sometimes happened during our journey that I was accosted by some one or other when unobserved, in places where we stopped. "Take care of that *angel keeper* of yours; if he did not belong to those *neri* (blacks), they would not have put him over you."

"There you are deceived," said I; "I have the greatest reason to believe that you are deceived."

"The most cunning," was the reply, "can always contrive to appear the most simple."

"If it were so, we ought never to give credit to the least goodness in any one."

"Yes, there are certain social stations," he replied, "in which men's manners may appear to great advantage by means of education; but as to virtue, they have none of it."

I could only answer, "You exaggerate, sir, you exaggerate."

"I am only consistent," he insisted. We were here interrupted, and I called to mind the *cave a consequentiariis* of Leibnitz.

Too many are inclined to adopt this false and terrible doctrine. I follow the standard A, that is JUSTICE. Another follows standard B; it must therefore be that of INJUSTICE, and, consequently, he must be a villain!

Give *me* none of your logical madness; whatever standard you adopt, do not reason so inhumanly. Consider, that by assuming what data you please, and procceding with the most violent stretch of rigour from one consequence to another, it is easy for any one to come to the conclusion that, "Beyond we four, all the rest of the world deserve to be burnt alive." And if we are at the pains of investigating a little further, we shall find each of the four crying out, "All deserve to be burnt alive together, with the exception of I myself."

This vulgar tenet of exclusiveness is in the highest degree unphilosophical. A moderate degree of suspicion is wise, but when urged to the extreme, it is the opposite.

After the hint thus thrown out to me respecting that *angelo custode*, I turned to study him with greater attention than I had before done; and each day served to convince me more and more of his friendly and generous nature.

When an order of society, more or less perfect, has been established, whether for better or worse, all the social offices, not pronounced by general consent to be infamous, all that are adapted to promote the public good, and the confidence of a respectable number, and which are filled by men acknowledged to be of upright mind, such offices may undeniably be undertaken by honest men without incurring any charge of unconscientiousness.

I have read of a Quaker who had a great horror of soldiers. He one day saw a soldier throw himself into the Thames, and save the life of a fellow-being who was drowning. "I don't care," he exclaimed, "I will still be a Quaker, but there are some good fellows, even among soldiers."

CHAPTER XCVIII.

STUNDBERGER accompanied me to my vehicle, into which I got with the brigadier of *gens d'armes*, to whose care I was entrusted. It was snowing, and the cold was excessive.

"Wrap yourself well up in your cloak," said Stundberger; "cover your head better, and contrive to reach home as little unwell as you can; remember, that a very little thing will give you cold just now. I wish it had been in my power to go on and attend you as far as Turin." He said this in a tone of voice so truly cordial and affectionate that I could not doubt its sincerity.

"From this time you will have no German near you," he added; "you will no longer hear our language spoken, and little, I dare say, will you care for that; the Italians find it very harsh. Besides, you have suffered so greatly among us, that most probably you will not like to remember us; yet, though you will so soon forget my very name, I shall not cease, sir, to offer up prayers for your safety."

"I shall do the same for you," I replied; as I shook his hand for the last time.

"Guten morgen! guten morgen! gute reise! leben sie wohl!"—farewell; a pleasant journey! good morning!—he continued to repeat; and the sounds were to me as sweet as if they had been pronounced in my native tongue.

I am passionately attached to my country, but I do not dislike any other nation. Civilisation, wealth, power, glory, are differently apportioned among different people; but in all there are minds obedient to the great vocation of man,—to love, to pity, and to assist each other.

The brigadier who attended me, informed me that he was one of those who arrested Confalonieri. He told me how the unhappy man had tried to make his escape; how he had been baffled, and how he had been torn from the arms of his distracted wife, while they both at the same time submitted to the calamity with dignity and resignation.

The horrible narrative increased my fear; a hand of iron seemed to be weighing upon my heart. The good man, in his desire of showing his sociality, and entertaining me with his remarks, was not aware of the horror he excited in me when I cast my eye on those hands which had seized the person of my unfortunate friend.

He ordered luncheon at Buffalora, but I was unable to taste anything. Many years back, when I was spending my time at Arluno, with the sons of Count Porro, I was accustomed to walk thither (to Buffalora), along the banks of the Ticino. I was rejoiced to see the noble bridge, the materials of which I had beheld scattered along the Lombard shore, now finished, notwithstanding the general opinion that the design would be abandoned. I rejoiced to traverse the river and set my foot once more on Piedmontese ground. With all my attachment to other nations, how much I prefer Italy! yet Heaven knows that however much more delightful to me is the sound of the *Italian name*, still sweeter must be that of Piedmont, the land of my fathers.

CHAPTER XCIX.

Opposite to Buffalora lies San Martino. Here the Lombard brigadier spoke of the Piedmontese carabineers, saluted me, and repassed the bridge.

"Let us go to Novara!" I said to the Vetturino.

"Have the goodness to stay a moment," said a carabineer. I found I was not yet free; and was much vexed, being apprehensive it would retard my arrival at the long-desired home. After waiting about a quarter of an hour, a gentleman came forward and requested to be allowed to accompany us as far as Novara. He had already missed one opportunity; there was no other conveyance than mine; and he expressed himself exceedingly happy that I permitted him to avail himself of it.

This carabineer in disguise was very good-humoured, and kept me company as far as Novara. Having reached that city, and feigning we were going to an hotel, he stopt at the barracks of the carabineers, and I was told there was a bed for me, and that I must wait the arrival of further orders. Concluding that I was to set off the next day, I went to bed, and after chatting some time with my host, I fell fast asleep; and it was long since I had slept so profoundly.

I awoke towards morning, rose as quickly as possible, and found the hours hang heavy on my hands. I took my breakfast, chatted, walked about the apartment and over the lodge, cast my eye over the host's books, and finally,—a visitor was announced. An officer had come to give me tidings respecting my father, and inform me that there was a letter from him, lying for me at Novara. I was exceedingly grateful to him for this act of humane courtesy. After a few hours, which to me appeared ages, I received my father's letter. Oh what joy to behold that hand-writing once more! what joy to learn that the best of mothers was spared to me! that my two brothers were alive, and also my eldest sister. Alas! my young and gentle Marietta, who had immured herself in the convent of the Visitazione, and of whom I had received so strange an account while a prisoner, had been dead upwards of nine months. It was a consolation for me to believe that I owed my liberty to all those who had never ceased to love and to pray for me, and more especially to a beloved sister who had died with every expression of the most edifying devotion. May the Almighty reward her for the many sufferings she underwent, and in particular for all the anxiety she experienced on my account.

Days passed on; yet no permission for me to quit Novara!

On the morning of the 16th of September, the desired order at length arrived, and all superintendence over me by the carabineers ceased. It seemed strange! so many years had now elapsed since I had been permitted to walk unaccompanied by guards. I recovered some money; I received the congratulations of some of my father's friends, and set out about three in the afternoon. The companions of my journey were a lady, a merchant, an engraver, and two young painters; one of whom was both deaf and dumb. These last were coming from Rome; and I was much pleased by hearing from them that they were acquainted with the family of my friend Maroncelli, for how pleasant a thing it is to be enabled to speak of those we love, with some one not wholly indifferent to them.

We passed the night at Vercelli. The happy day, the 17th of September, dawned at last. We pursued our journey; and how slow we appeared to travel! it was evening before we arrived at Turin.

Who would attempt to describe the consolation I felt; the nameless feelings of delight, when I found myself in the embraces of my father, my mother, and my two brothers? My dear sister Giuseppina was not then with them; she was fulfilling her duties at Chieri; but on hearing of my felicity, she hastened to stay for a few days with our family, to make it complete. Restored to these five long-sighed-for, and beloved objects of my tenderness, —I was, and I still am, one of the most enviable of mankind.

Now, therefore, for all my past misfortunes and sufferings, as well as for all the good or evil yet reserved for me, may the providence of God be blessed; of God, who renders all men, and all things, however opposite the intentions of the actors, the wonderful instruments which He directs to the greatest and best of purposes.

www.ingramcontent.com/pod-product-compliance
Lightning Source LLC
Chambersburg PA
CBHW030541040726
47497CB00008B/2548
* 9 7 8 3 7 4 4 7 5 1 2 5 4 *